To See Him Face to Face

Second Edition

Cindy Hamilton

To my family past, present, and into God's future.

Jesus also did many other things. If they were all written down, I suppose the whole world could not contain the books that would be written.
--John 21:25 (NLT)

Contents

Title Page

Copyright

Dedication

Preface

Mary   1

James, the Brother of Jesus   32

Interlude One   63

The Baptist   64

The Calling of Simon and Andrew   78

Peter's Mother-in-Law   82

The Wedding at Cana   105

The Healing of the Paralytic   111

The Calling of Levi   115

Andrew and the Boy with the Loaves and Fishes   118

Leah   122

The Parable of the Workers in the Vineyard   131

Interlude Two   134

The Prostitute   135

The Banquet   139

The Ten Lepers   141

The Woman at the Well   145

The Blind Man   150

Zacchaeus   153

Interlude Three   156

The Woman from Syria Phoenicia   157

Mary and Martha   168

The Transfiguration   181

Interlude Four   188

Mary Magdalene   189

John   210

Peter   217

Simon of Cyrene   221

Questions   230

Write Your Own Story   240

Jesus and the Children   243

The Sower   247

Bibles   251

Acknowledgement   253

About The Author   255

Books By This Author   257

Preface

The Bible says, *"Jesus Christ is the same yesterday, today, and forever"* (Hebrews 13:8). The Jesus that lived and walked in the land we call Israel is the same Jesus that lives within me today. He is the same Jesus who laughed with the disciples, delivered Mary Magdalene of the seven demons, and raised Lazarus from the dead. Who were these people? Sometimes their stories become so familiar that they lose their effect on us. How do we apply their stories to our lives today in the 21st century?

In her book, *The Soul at Rest*, Tricia McCary Rhodes describes a contemplative practice called scripture praying. "We step into the Bible's pictures, parables, and encounters with God, like participants in a story where the ink on the pages hasn't had time to dry. The Author is there to meet us. This experience opens our eyes to horizons we've never scanned." She continues by quoting A.W. Tozer who wrote, "A new world arises out of the religious mists when we approach our Bible with the idea that it is not only a book that was once spoken, but a book that is now speaking."

Even as a child, I had a deep yearning to know God. Blessed with a vivid imagination, I often wondered what it would be like to see Jesus and sit down and talk to him face to face. Eighteen years ago, I began the practice of scripture praying. This enriched and blessed my time with God, opening up the Bible in ways that I never thought possible, and best of all, allowed me to glimpse the face of Jesus. I've seen him smile . . . and frown. I've felt His touch on my shoulder, listened to His stories, and even looked into His eyes.

Even now, morning is my time with God, often waking before the alarm, anticipating the conversation with my Father and that first cup of coffee. I have a special chair that I sit in that is flanked on both sides by end tables strewn with an assortment of Bibles, books, and commentaries. I call it my "prayer chair". Back in 2003, Ruby, the dachshund, and Tess, the Siamese, rose early with me. They often joined me with Ruby sandwiched at my side and Tess curled up by my neck on the top of the chair. Settling down, I was transported into the very Presence of the Father by opening His book and feasting on the stories within. These mornings, I am joined by Wynna, the terrier, and Max the dachshund.

Years ago, I began by writing short vignettes in my journal, stories taken from the parables of Jesus or the people in His life. Writing in the first person allowed me to walk their walk with him. As the stories continued, I began to write longer ones, simply because, like reading a good book, I didn't want the stories to end. One story might have taken several months to write. As the story unfolded, I would often meditate on one line of scripture in the story, praying over it, asking God what He wanted me to learn. He often would show me other scriptures that pertained to it, teaching me something new each week. Finally, He would allow me to move the story along.

The most beautiful part of this process was the

feelings that were evoked within me as these scriptures came to life. I found myself laughing with the disciples over one of Jesus' stories, or crying with Mary because Jesus did not come and heal her brother. These people became so real to me. They had real emotions when they encountered Jesus. As they embraced him, so did I. I would take these feelings, thoughts, and images from God and use them to strengthen me for the coming day.

In 2003, I was a school counselor. In my job, I often encountered students and others who desperately needed to feel a special touch from Jesus. Even though I could not speak to them of him, is presence was so real within me from my time spent with Jesus each morning that I felt him reaching out to them through me.

Jesus is the same today. He wants to become real to his children and not remain a character in a storybook that is placed on a shelf and dusted off now and then.

Anyone can meet God in this powerful and personal way. Scripture praying is a wonderful tool that Christians can use to unlock the mysteries of God—and to meet him face to face.

I wanted to update *To See Him Face to Face* in a fresh way by adding a couple of more stories, editing it a little more, and adding a Bible Study at the end. I still approach the Bible in this way as I read the stories in the Old and New Testaments. It never gets old but has blessed me so much throughout the years. A lot has happened in the last thirteen years, but Jesus has been faithful and so real to me. I still meet him every morning as a friend, confiding in him, and talking to him face to face. A friend once said, "I want to walk so close to Jesus that when I die, I will keep right on walking with him." That's what I want too.

These stories are created from my love for Christ with an unfathomable yearning *To See Him Face to Face.*

Soli Deo Gloria (Glory to God Alone)

Mary

Chapter One

Luke 1 & 2; Matthew 1 & 2

❙❙ Mary, come quickly!" I put down the piece of cloth that I was sewing and hurried toward the sound of my mother's voice. When I walked into the other room, Mother beckoned for me to come sit down beside her. Father stood to her left. They both beamed with pleasure.

"Mother, Father, what is it?" I asked smiling at them both.

"Your father has wonderful news, Mary."

My mother's sweet, beautiful face looked with love at my father. He smiled at her then took my hand. "Mary, I have found you a husband," he said proudly. "I have talked to the matchmaker, and we both feel that this man will be perfect for you."

I admit that I was stunned. Of course, I was of the age to get married, but I had not really let myself consider the possibility of leaving my mother and my father.

"Who is he, Father?" I asked curiously.

"Joseph, the carpenter," he replied.

My mother added, "He is a very kind man, my child. He will be good to you."

I nodded obediently as I thought about the man

who was to be my husband. He seemed so old. My mother had begun to teach me the ways of a man and wife. I blushed as I thought about it. I quickly put that thought out of my mind, as I knew that I had at least a year of betrothal before this was expected of me.

"When will the ceremony be, Father?"

"I have talked to Joseph, and he hopes it will take place within the month," my father explained.

There was so much to do to prepare for the ceremony, but we were betrothed in front of our family and friends three weeks later. We would now have a year to get to know each other.

I found that Joseph was truly a kind and patient man. He was not a large man, but he was strong as an ox. I could not help but watch him, as he carried wood into his workshop, his muscles taut from the exertion.

We laughed a lot together. He had an exceptional sense of humor and kept me entertained as he worked by telling me stories. One story he loved to tell was about a rich lady from the village who hired him to build some new furniture. She had gone to Jerusalem and brought back the latest designs. As he worked, however, she kept changing her mind until the end product looked exactly like the furniture she had in the first place. He would laugh his huge laugh; enjoying the story more each time he told it.

Joseph also loved God. One day, we were walking together in a field outside of the village. We stopped underneath an ancient, gnarled olive tree.

"Mary, look at this tree, how twisted and ugly it is," he said.

I walked up to the tree and ran my fingers down its rough bark.

Joseph continued, "But, how blessed I am that God has given me the gift to turn this wood into something of beauty. Tomorrow I will return and cut it down and haul it back to the shop. I plan to craft this tree into a beautiful table for our new home."

Gradually I began to love this sweet, funny man. I looked forward to the time we would become man and wife.

Several weeks later, the village rabbi and my father were talking together. The rabbi had come from Jerusalem with some interesting news. Father came home immediately and shared the incredible story with mother and me.

Father told us that his cousin, Zechariah, had seen a vision at the temple. The rabbi had told Father that he was praying with a group of men outside the temple during the hour of incense. Zechariah had gone inside to do his duty and did not come out for a very long time. The men praying outside could not understand what was taking him so long.

When Zechariah finally appeared, the men perceived that he had seen a vision. He was as white as the pillar he stood beside, and his eyes were dilated as if he were in shock. He opened his mouth as if to speak and nothing came out! The rabbi told Father that Zechariah stayed in Jerusalem until the duration of his service was completed and then left immediately to return to his wife, Elizabeth, in the hills of Judah.

My mother and I listened raptly. What could God be doing in Zechariah's life? Later, I shared the story with Joseph. He was as amazed and fascinated as we had been.

*****

March was here and with it the warm, fragrant winds of spring. I decided to take a walk early one morning. Spring was my favorite time of year. I enjoyed walking through the rocky fields, seeing the flowers push their way up through the thin soil. I marveled that flowers so lovely could grow in such poor conditions.

This morning was especially beautiful. The sky fanned out in front of me in shades of pink and blue, bathing the field in hues of pastels. As I was walking, I paused because I thought I heard someone calling my name. Stopping, I looked around. Seeing nothing, I continued my walk. Once again, I heard the soft sound. Perhaps it was the wind.

I decided to rest for a moment on a hill overlooking Nazareth. Sitting down, I felt the wind begin to blow again, stronger this time. I reached up to grab the scarf that was around my head, holding it close beneath my chin. Closing my eyes, I heard someone call my name one more time.

"Mary, rejoice highly favored one, the Lord is with you; blessed are you among women!"

Opening my eyes, I saw an angel standing in front of me. My first reaction was fear. Drawing back from the vision, I hid my eyes behind the scarf that I had wrapped close to my head.

"Do not be afraid, Mary, for you have found favor with God."

Peeking out from behind the scarf, I dared to look at the angel in front of me. He was beautiful, tall and straight, clothed in a robe that actually glistened. He was smiling at me.

"And behold, you will conceive in your womb and bring forth a Son and shall call His name, JESUS."

"He will be great, and will be called the Son of the Highest, and the Lord God will give Him the throne of His father David."

"And He will reign over the house of Jacob forever and of His Kingdom, there will be no end."

Forgetting my fear, I looked at the angel in disbelief. What was he saying? What did this mean?

"How can this be," I objected. "I am a virgin." I knew enough of my mother's lessons to know this was impossible.

The angel explained with a patient and quiet voice. "Mary, *the Holy Spirit will come upon you, and the power of the Highest will overshadow you; therefore, also, that Holy One who is to be born will be called the Son of God."*

Before I could think through what the angel had said, he said one more incredible thing. *"Now indeed, Elizabeth, your relative has also conceived a son in her old age; and she is in her sixth month of pregnancy."*

Elizabeth is pregnant? But she is barren. I was astounded at this news, also. This cannot be possible. She and Zechariah grieved over her barrenness.

As if reading my thoughts, the angel smiled once again and said, "Mary, *with God, nothing is impossible."*

I closed my eyes one more time trying to sort out all that the angel had told me. Finally, I opened my eyes and asked, "What is your name?"

"I am Gabriel," he said.

No longer afraid, I felt an incredible sense of peace and love. In a quiet, yet firm voice, I looked up at him and said, "Gabriel, I am here to serve the Lord. I will carry His child."

With a brilliant smile, he raised his wings and vanished as quickly and quietly as he had appeared.

I sat there for at least an hour. The early morning had turned into a beautiful day. What was I to do now? Should I tell my parents? What about Joseph? Would he understand? Fear began to creep in as I tried to think through all of the questions that were running through my mind.

"Lord, God, please lead me. Tell me what to do now."

And then I remembered what the angel had said, *"Elizabeth, your kinsmen, has also conceived and in her sixth month of pregnancy."* Elizabeth! Of course, I must go to Elizabeth. She will understand.

I walked slowly home, going over and over in my mind all the things that the angel had said to me. I sought out my mother as soon as I came into the house. I found her standing by the fire, beginning to prepare the noonday meal.

"Mother," I said quietly.

"Mary, where have you been?" she answered. "I have been looking for you."

My mother turned toward me and stopped. There was a look of surprise and concern on her face.

"Are you feeling unwell?" My mother hurried over to me and placed her cool hand on my brow.

"Sit down, child. You are so pale."

I did as she said, grateful for the normalcy of her motherly concern. I was not sure what to tell my mother. Struggling to come up with the right words, I said, "Mother, something has happened to me that I cannot explain right now. Please trust that what I am asking to do will someday make sense to you."

"What is it, child?" my mother asked worriedly.

"I must go see Elizabeth and Zechariah," I answered.

I have always been an obedient and trustworthy child, never giving my parents a moment of concern. My mother had no reason to doubt my sincerity or my words.

Trusting me and not understanding why, she said, "We will speak to your father and Joseph."

That evening, I sat down with my mother and father and tried to explain what had happened to me. After I finished my story, my father stood up and walked to the door. He stood there for several minutes, looking out, but seeing nothing in the street. Finally, he turned around and looked at my mother and then at me. There were tears in his eyes as he said, "Mary, do you understand what all of this means to you?"

I bowed my head as he continued.

"There are many who will not believe your story. Joseph will probably choose to break your engagement."

I nodded, understanding exactly what my father was saying. I had not yet taken the time to consider how this would impact Joseph.

"Father, what am I to do?" I asked tearfully.

"We will tell him that you would like to visit your kinswoman, Elizabeth, during this happy time in her life. This will give you time to think through all that has happened," he said.

I nodded, grateful to my father for the trust he had in me.

When I missed my cycle later that month, I knew it was time to go and stay with Elizabeth and Zechariah. My mother helped me prepare for the journey.

Before I left, I went by Joseph's shop to tell him good-bye. When I walked in the door, I heard him whistle that funny little tune that he liked so much. He was working intently on our beautiful table.

"Mary!" His handsome face lit up as I walked into the room. "You are looking especially beautiful this morning."

I blushed and smiled. "Joseph, it is time for me to go."

He put down his tools and walked around the table to me. Putting his arm around my shoulders, he said, 'I will miss you, Mary. When are you returning?"

"I am not sure how long that I will stay with Elizabeth."

Joseph must have sensed hesitancy in my voice. He took me by both shoulders and turned me around to face him. "Mary, are you alright? I sense that something is troubling you."

Tears sprang to my eyes as I looked into his face.

"Joseph, I will tell you everything when I return from Elizabeth's."

He looked intently at me for a moment as if to reassure himself that everything was all right. I smiled at him and gave him a quick hug.

"I must go. Father is waiting for me."

I left him standing there, still a look of confusion on his face.

*****

Father was waiting outside the house, the donkey packed with things that we would need for our short journey. The journey was pleasant enough. Father said very little to me, keeping his thoughts to himself. As for me, I thought again and again about what the angel had said. We arrived at Zechariah's house late into the evening on the following day. Zechariah met us at the door. He was beaming.

"Zechariah, you are looking well," said Father.

Without a word, he embraced Father and me and motioned for us to come into the house. Exchanging curious glances with each other, Father and I followed him. Zechariah immediately began to move around the room, putting out chairs for us and gesturing for us to sit down. He pointed to the next room and then left us.

"Father, why is Zechariah not speaking?"

"I do not know, child. This is indeed strange."

We waited quietly for a few minutes. Presently Zechariah returned with Elizabeth following close behind.

Father and I stood up when she entered. Seeing her smiling face, I called out to her, "Greetings, Elizabeth!"

At the moment of the greeting, Elizabeth froze, caught her breath, and placed her hand on her abdomen. Her beautiful face now showed a mixture of awe and surprise.

Zechariah took hold of her arm in concern. She looked at him, smiled, and patted his hand on her arm. Looking back at me, tears filled her eyes and she said, *"Blessed are you among women, and blessed is the fruit of your womb. Why is it granted to me that the mother of my Lord should come to me?* Mary, *at the sound of your greeting, the babe leaped in my womb for joy!"*

"Blessed are you because you believed what God has told you. And now it will be fulfilled within you."

If ever I needed confirmation of all that had happened, this was it. Elizabeth spoke to my heart through the inspiration of the Holy Spirit. I was overtaken by a sense of love that was so powerful that I had to sit down before I collapsed.

I bowed my head, my spirit feeling as if it would burst out of me in joy. I opened my mouth to speak and said,

"My soul glorifies the Lord
and my spirit rejoices in God my Savior,
for he has been mindful
of the humble state of his servant.
From now on all generations will call me blessed,
for the Mighty One has done great things for me—
holy is his name.
His mercy extends to those who fear him,
from generation to generation.
He has performed mighty deeds with his arm;
he has scattered those who are proud in their inmost
thoughts.
He has brought down rulers from their thrones
but has lifted up the humble.
He has filled the hungry with good things
but has sent the rich away empty.
He has helped his servant Israel,
remembering to be merciful
to Abraham and his descendants forever,
just as he promised our ancestors" (Luke 1:46-55 NIV).

There was silence for a while after I spoke these words. We all sat there basking in the love of the Holy Spirit.

Finally, my father stood up and came over to me. "I will leave now my child. It seems that you are in good hands here. May God take care of you."

I looked up at my father. He softly laid his hand on

my head. At his touch, I began to cry, huge wracking sobs coming from deep within my soul. At that moment, I was a child, my father's little girl, truly overwhelmed by all that was about to happen to me."

Gathering me in his arms, my father allowed me to cry it out. When nothing was left and my crying had ended, my father said, "Mary, God will protect and take care of you. You must be a very special girl for him to have chosen you."

Strengthened now, I stood back from my father and smiled. "Yes, Father, He will take care of me."

I stayed with Elizabeth and Zechariah for three months. Each day was precious. Since Zechariah could not speak, Elizabeth enjoyed my company. We talked often about our sons and what their lives would be like.

At the end of three months, I knew it was time to go home and face Joseph. God had indeed strengthened me during my stay with Elizabeth.

My father came to get me soon after. I hugged Elizabeth good-bye, her huge belly getting in the way. We laughed and cried together one more time. Elizabeth looked at me, her kind face showing her love and concern.

"Mary, you will be constantly in my prayers. May God go with you."

I hugged her one more time. "And may God be with you, Elizabeth."

*****

Returning home, I knew I must go immediately to Joseph's shop to talk to him. I found him at work, whistling as he sanded a little child's chair.

"Mary!" Joseph called when he spotted me standing at the door. He came towards me, wiping his hands on a rag. "Your home. When did you come?"

Smiling at him, I said, "Father and I arrived yesterday evening."

"Come and sit down." He wiped off a bench with the rag that he held in his hand. After we both sat down, he asked about Elizabeth and Zechariah.

"She is soon to give birth, Joseph. Zechariah still cannot speak, but he walks around beaming at everyone."

Joseph laughed and said, "Yes, he must be very proud of himself."

There was silence between us as we both thought about Elizabeth and Zechariah. Breaking the silence, I said, "Joseph, there is something I must tell you."

Joseph looked at me seriously. "Yes, Mary, you mentioned something before you left to visit Elizabeth. I have wondered what it might be."

I had rehearsed what I would say a hundred times in the last three months. Now, sitting here with Joseph, I had a difficult time even knowing how to begin.

Joseph reached out and took my hand. "What is it, Mary? You can tell me anything." The love in his voice gave me courage. I took a deep breath and began my story, starting with my walk that day and the angel appearing to me.

"Joseph, I am three months pregnant," I said softly.

Joseph looked at me with a look that I could not identify. He stood up and walked to the other side of the room, his back to me.

When he did not speak, I asked him fearfully, "Joseph, do you not believe me?" He still did not speak. I called his name one more time, "Joseph?" He turned toward me. There was anguish in his voice when he spoke. "Mary, I do not know what to think."

Tears welled up in my eyes when I realized that Joseph might not believe me. If he does not, it is his right to divorce me. I could not allow myself to even consider what would happen to me then.

I turned to go. The pain in my heart was so intense that I could not stay in that room one more minute. Joseph did not stop me as I walked out of the door. I did not know where I was going; I had to get away from Joseph. I walked back to the place that the angel had spoken to me.

"Lord, God, where are you? Where are you, Gabriel? God, what am I going to do now? " I cried out to God, but there was only silence. Doubt and fear began to creep over me. As the day began to fade, I walked home slowly.

My mother met me at the door. She knew by the look on my face that my conversation with Joseph had not gone well. Taking me in her arms, I cried. Finally, my mother said, "Child, your father and I will not desert you. We will be here for you." Taking some assurance in that, I tried to smile at her.

Several days passed. Somehow, I got through them by going about all of the mundane tasks that I must do– washing, cooking, and sewing. I moved leadenly through the days, not allowing myself to think beyond the next hour.

One evening, three days later, I was sitting outside the house trying to make use of the last little bit of light as I mended one of my father's shirts. I heard someone approach. Looking up from my task, I saw Joseph walking towards me. Not wanting to speak to him, I quickly gathered my sewing to go inside.

"Mary, don't go." There was a pleading in his voice that caused me to pause. "Mary, I must speak to you," he insisted. "Please, put your sewing down and come with me."

I hesitated, but the look that he gave me encouraged me to do as he said. We walked together out of the village to the olive grove where we had gone so many times before to talk.

I remember being so aware of the fragrant and warm summer air. It was early evening, and the summer sun was just now settling down in the sky.

I did not speak to him. I'd said it all. We sat down on a boulder still warm from the day. Joseph wasted no time, but began by saying,

"Mary, I am sorry that I did not believe you."

I looked at him in surprise, still not speaking.

"After you told me that you were pregnant, I did not know what to do. I did not want to make you a public example, so I decided that I would secretly divorce you. I thought perhaps you could go back to Elizabeth's to have the baby."

"Last night I went to sleep with all of this on my mind. Mary, God sent an angel to speak to me in a dream. Perhaps it was the same angel who spoke to you. The angel told me, *'Joseph, Son of David, do not be afraid to take to you Mary your wife, for that which is conceived in her is of the Holy Spirit.'* Matthew 1:20, 21

Joseph stopped speaking, overwhelmed by his emotions. By this time, we were both crying.

"And the angel told me that you would bring forth a son, and I will name him Jesus, for He will save his people from their sins."

Joseph looked at me in awe and said, "Mary, God has chosen us to raise his child." He gathered me in his arms and held me. How grateful I was that God had not asked me to do this all by myself. He has given me a man who will walk this amazing road by my side. It will take both of us to raise God's son.

We walked hand in hand back to the village, making plans, talking about the future.

We were legally married two days later. I left my mother and father's house to live with Joseph as his wife. There were questions around the village, but Joseph was such a respected man that the gossip soon died down.

My pregnancy went well. I was not troubled by the sickness that other women have when they are pregnant. The angel did not visit us again, but Joseph and I were very aware of God's presence in our lives.

We had heard that Elizabeth and Zechariah had delivered a son. Joseph came home one day to tell me the strange story. He said that on the eighth day, Zechariah (who still could not speak) went to the synagogue to circumcise the baby. The priest was going to call the child, Zechariah.

Elizabeth answered and said that the child's name was John. The priest looked at her strangely and said there was no one in the family by that name.

Shaking his head and frowning, the priest made signs to Zechariah. Surely, Zechariah would straighten this out. Zechariah called for a writing tablet, and wrote, *"His name is John."*

Immediately, Zechariah's tongue was loosed, and he spoke praising God and prophesying that this child would be called *"the Prophet of the Highest, and he would go before the face of the Lord to prepare His way."*

Later that evening, Joseph and I spoke of Elizabeth and Zechariah's child. It was still so difficult for us to understand the enormity of all that was happening. Joseph and I wondered what our blessed child would be like. What would he look like? All parents have these thoughts before a child is born, but this child was God's very own Son.

*****

The next few months were very quiet and peaceful for Joseph and me. We had settled in together, comfortable in our life with each other. The baby was very active within me. He would move vigorously at night, and I would wake up thinking of him and praying to His Father. My baby's father was God, himself. As I lay in bed, feeling the baby move, I would be so aware of an enormous outflowing of love in and around me.

One evening, Joseph came home with unsettling news. A decree had gone out from Caesar Augustus that all of the Roman world would be taxed. The Romans ask what they will with no concern for the people. They always need more money to build their armies and their roads. Now it seems that we were to go from Nazareth to the City of David in Bethlehem because that was where Joseph was born and registered.

"Mary, you must stay here with your mother and father," Joseph told me. I could tell that he had thought through this plan carefully. "The journey would be too difficult for you. It is soon time for the baby to arrive. You must be with your mother so that she can help with the birth." His kind eyes looked at me with love and concern.

I shook my head. "No, Joseph. I must go with you." I guess my firmness surprised him.

"But what if the babe arrives while we are on the journey?"

"Then God will help us. I feel very strongly that I must be with you when the baby comes."

We left two weeks later. Joseph had packed our donkey with the needed provisions, including those things we might need for the birth of the baby.

I did not realize how difficult this journey would be for me. We progressed very slowly, Joseph walking and leading our little donkey with me riding. I tried not to complain but would have to stop often to rest and stretch my legs. At times I would walk beside Joseph in comfortable silence, neither of us feeling the need to talk.

At night I would try to rest, curled on my side on a pallet on the ground, secure in knowing that Joseph was watching out for our safety.

We encountered many travelers along the way. There was a lot of grumbling and complaining toward the Roman government. People were angry that they had to make this journey. As always, in difficult times like this, people would wish for the promised Messiah to come. "He" would save them from the Roman oppressors.

In the evening around a small fire, Joseph and I would sit and talk.

"Joseph?" I said quietly staring at the warm flames. "Yes?"

"Will our child be the Messiah? Will he be the one that will overthrow the Roman oppressors? I cannot bear to think of him in this role as a warrior or conqueror."

Joseph did not answer me for a while. He, too,

stared into the fire. "I don't know," he said honestly. "The angel told me that his name is Jesus, and he will save his people from their sins. The angel did not tell me that he will save us from the Romans."

The next morning, we rose early. I was so stiff and sore that I could barely walk. Joseph smiled at me in sympathy. "It will not be long," he said kindly. "Can you make it one more day? Surely, we will be able to find a nice inn with a soft, comfortable pallet for you to rest on."

I nodded, praying that God would give me the strength I needed for the rest of the journey.

We arrived in Bethlehem late that evening. The little town was bursting with activity, full of travelers that had come from all over the area in order to be counted in the census.

Joseph found a quiet place by the well for me to rest.

"Stay here while I go and see if I can find a place for us to stay tonight."

I smiled gratefully at him and sat down on the well holding tightly to the reins of our little donkey. On his back were all of our precious possessions.

Joseph was gone for over an hour. I began to worry about him, wondering what was keeping him so long. He finally appeared, shaking his head. "I have gone from inn to inn. They are all full. The only thing I could find was a stable attached to an inn at the edge of town. The innkeeper said that we could bed down there."

I was so tired at that point that I honestly didn't care where we slept. I just wanted to rest. The baby had been very quiet all day, but my back was beginning to hurt.

I tried to smile bravely at him and said, "That will

be fine. Perhaps we can find someplace in a few days when the crowds clear out."

We made our way slowly to the stable. When we got there, I peeked in through the door to take a look at our home for the next few days. It was dark and very dusty. There were animals already bedded down for the night. Luckily, the innkeeper had brought in a fresh pile of hay in anticipation of the guests for the night. Joseph began to make a little nest for us. We had brought a blanket from home, which we laid on top of the bed. We both eased down on the soft bed and closed our eyes, too tired to talk or even eat.

Later that night, I dreamed that I was still riding on our donkey. My back was hurting so bad. I woke up sweating despite the cool night air. I turned on my side, hoping to relieve the pain. It eased up for a while, then started hurting again. I sat up, hoping this new position would help me feel better. When I did, I experienced a huge amount of wetness between my legs. Alarmed for a moment, I sat still trying to understand what was happening. Then it came to me, a knowing that was as old as time itself. I was in labor! The baby was soon to be born.

Joseph stirred beside me. "Joseph," I whispered. "The baby is coming." He rolled over toward me.

"What did you say?" He asked sleepily.

"The baby—I'm in labor."

Joseph sat up immediately. "Lord, Jehovah, help us!

"Yes, Joseph. He will."

Surprisingly, I did not panic, even though there was no mid-wife to help me through my labors. Joseph never left my side. He talked me through the difficult pains, reassuring me that everything would be all right. He prayed to God that I might deliver my son easily and quickly.

*****

Early in the morning hours of the night, my son was born. With Joseph holding my shoulders, I pushed my beautiful baby boy into the world. He came out crying, drawing in great gulps of life-giving air.

Joseph and I cried with him, cries of joy. We experienced the most incredible feeling of love and well-being.

Joseph gently washed the baby off from the water that he had drawn from the nearby well. Jesus squalled lustily through the entire process. Finally, wrapped tight in a warm blanket, Joseph handed the precious bundle to me. I held him to my breast where nature took over, and he began to nurse.

He was beautiful. He had a head full of black hair and soft olive-colored skin tinted a rosy pink. I could not take my eyes from him. He did not nurse long but soon fell asleep in my arms. Joseph had cleaned out a small feeding trough and filled it with clean, sweet-smelling hay. He took Jesus from me and placed him gently into the rough little bed. He drew the bed close by my side so that I could easily reach out to him when he cried.

We slept. I was so tired from the journey and the birth of my son. Joseph and I curled up together in the hay, our beautiful baby asleep close by.

Several hours later, a commotion outside the manger woke Joseph with a start. Alerted for possible danger, he grabbed a staff nearby and went quickly to the door. Unbelievably, outside the manger, a rag-tag group of dirty and smelly shepherds was standing quietly, almost apologetically. When they saw Joseph, the leader of the group stepped forward.

Respectfully, he said, "Sir please excuse the intrusion, but we had to know if a babe was born to you and your wife tonight."

Astonished, Joseph looked at each one of the men. He saw wonder, awe—even reverence in their faces. Without speaking, Joseph nodded his head. The men let out almost a collective sigh, their dark faces wreathed in smiles.

The leader of the group spoke. "My brothers and I were out in the fields, keeping watch over our flocks. We were wrapped in our blankets, gathered around a dying fire. Suddenly an angel of the Lord stood in front of us, and we were surrounded by glorious light. At first, we were terrified, not understanding what was happening. The angel spoke to us and told us not to be afraid, for he had brought good news to us and all people."

"For there is born to you this day in the City of David, a Savior, who is Christ the Lord. And this will be a sign to you. You will find a Babe wrapped in swaddling clothes, lying in a manger."

"Suddenly, we heard the most beautiful music. Looking up, the sky was full of angels singing and praising God."

*"Glory to God in the highest
And on earth, peace Goodwill
Toward men"* (Luke 2:11-14).

"We were on our feet by this time, totally unafraid. The sight was too glorious to behold. There were thousands of angels. Wherever we turned to look, there were angels—a symphony of angels!"

"We don't know how long we stood there, our hearts pounding, and our mouths gaped open in awe.

But the angels disappeared as quickly as they appeared. When we looked from the sky back to the messenger angel, he was gone, also."

"We stood there silently, not speaking for a long time. Finally, we dared to look at each other. I spoke first. *"Let us go to Bethlehem and see this thing that has come to pass which the Lord has made known to us."*

"My brothers agreed, so we left our flocks with our little brother and hurried here to Bethlehem as quickly as we could."

Convinced of the story and believing these men meant the baby and me no harm, Joseph invited the shepherds to come into the stable.

He gently woke me and explained that a marvelous thing had happened to these men. The story of the angels was recounted for me.

I tenderly lifted the baby out of his warm little bed and gave him to Joseph. With pride, Joseph carried Jesus in his arms over to the group of shepherds.

They smiled and nodded, praising God for this beautiful male child, still in awe of all that had happened. The leader requested from Joseph that he might hold the babe. Joseph looked at me, and I nodded. As Joseph placed the child in the shepherd's arms, tears streamed down his weathered, leathery cheeks. The others gathered around him, touched as well.

I sat there quietly, watching the men worship my son. He was so tiny and vulnerable. This baby, my baby, was the Savior—the Christ. Angels proclaimed his birth to these lowly shepherds. I held my thoughts close to my heart, sealed with the first of many prayers for my son. "Lord God help me to be a good mother to your son. Help me to be worthy of your trust."

The shepherds left the stable calling out in the night, "Praise God! Glory to God!" I am surprised that they did not wake up the entire neighborhood.

After they left, Joseph brought Jesus back to me. I held him close to nurse one more time until I found myself nodding off. Joseph took the baby gently from me and laid him back in the manger.

*****

We woke up early in the morning to the sound of the baby rooting around in his crib and the animals beginning to stir. A traveler came in to get his donkey to begin his day's journey. Surprised when he saw us, he quickly bridled his animal and left.

"Mary, we must find another place to stay tonight. I will go out one more time to look. Will you be all right?

I assured him that the baby and I would be fine.

Joseph came back several hours later, smiling and quite pleased with himself. He had run into a gentleman who needed the services of a carpenter. The man also knew of a small house that we could rent that was close by.

Thrilled to leave the dusty and grimy stable, we gathered our belongings and moved to the little house. Praising God for our good fortune, we settled in. It was small, but at least it did not have the smell of a stable.

Eight days after his birth, Joseph took the baby to the temple in Bethlehem to be circumcised. I, of course, could not yet leave the house. I could only pace and worry as women over the centuries have done, knowing and understanding the necessity of the ancient rite, yet hating it also.

Joseph brought the baby back to me several hours later. He was smiling and said, "He is fine, Mary, just very hungry." He carefully placed Jesus in my arms. I smiled up at Joseph, grateful to have my baby safe in my arms again.

My thirty-three days of purification went by quickly. I blissfully worked around the house, enjoying this quiet time with Joseph and the baby. Jesus was a good baby, only crying when he was hungry or wet. Since Joseph was working close by, he would often stop in during the day to check on us.

All too soon, it was time to leave the house and take Jesus to Jerusalem to present him to the Lord. We had saved our money so that we could purchase two pigeons for my purification sacrifice and five shekels to redeem our little son.

We walked reverently into the temple courtyard. I was carrying Jesus, and Joseph was carrying the cage with the two pigeons. Not ever having done this before, Joseph was not sure what we were to do or where we were to go. He spotted a man sitting on the temple steps and said to me, "Mary, I will go and ask that man where we are to go." He looks as if he is waiting for someone. Perhaps he can tell us what we are to do."

I smiled at Joseph and waited. Jesus had awakened by that time. His beautiful little dark eyes were open, and he began looking around. As a mother would do, I began talking to him. "Jesus, you are in your Father's house. Isn't it beautiful?" I held him up as if to see.

At that moment, Joseph walked back to us with the man following close behind. The man had a strange look on his face as he glanced at me and then at Jesus.

"Mary, this is Simeon." Simeon had eyes only for the baby. In a trembling voice, he asked if he might hold

Jesus. I looked at Joseph. He smiled his consent. Looking back at the old man, I carefully placed Jesus in his arms. Tears ran down his face as he looked at the child. Jesus looked back at Simeon with the solemn stare of a baby.

Simeon blessed God and said,
*"Sovereign Lord, now let your servant die in peace,
as you have promised.
I have seen your salvation,
which you have prepared for all people.
He is a light to reveal God to the nations,
and he is the glory of your people Israel!"*
Luke 2:29-32 (NLT)

Joseph and I marveled at what he said. The three of us continued to stand and look at the beautiful baby nestled in Simeon's arms. Simeon's words, "a light to the gentiles" continued to ring in my ears. How many people have now spoken of this little baby---Gabriel, Martha, the angels in the field, the shepherds, and now this dear old man?

Simeon tenderly placed the baby back in my arms, his face now wreathed in a smile. He raised his gnarled hand and blessed Joseph and me. Then Simeon's voice changed, and he did an unusual and comfortable thing, especially for a Jewish man. He looked directly at me and said very gently, *"Behold this Child is destined for the fall and rising of many in Israel, and for a sign which will be spoken against (yes, a sword will pierce through your own soul also), that the thoughts of many hearts may be revealed"* (Matthew 2:34, 35).

Suddenly, the happiness of the day disappeared. What did this old man mean? Fearfully, I hugged Jesus closer to me. All the words and prophecies spoken about my baby up to now have been joyous and uplifting.

Instinctively I began backing away from the old man and his fearful words. As I turned away, I found myself face to face with an old lady, bent over with age. Her sweet, wrinkled face and kind eyes comforted my soul as if my mother were standing there. She must have walked up as we were speaking to Simeon. She gently put her arm around me, sensing my fear. In a beautiful, melodious voice, she began singing and praising God. The music touched my soul and eased my fear. I smiled at her. She told me that her name was Anna. She had been married seven years and a widow for eighty-four. She never left the temple area but worshipped there night and day. Her face reflected the joy that was in her soul. Like a balm, her joy replaced the fear that was in my heart.

Listening to her life story, one of sorrow and joy, I knew that God would be with me and give me the strength, courage, and wisdom that I would need to raise His Son.

*****

We returned to Bethlehem for two more years. Joseph continued his carpentry work, and I settled in, loving my role as wife and mother. Jesus was a delightful baby. His smiles melted me, and I would sit for hours on the floor and play with him. Jesus adored Joseph. His eyes would light up when Joseph came through the door each evening. Jesus would laugh, throw up his arms, and babble until Joseph picked him up and swung him around the room. We were so happy.

Little did I know that our idyllic life was about to change. One day when Jesus was close to two years old, Joseph had come home from work early. We were all sitting in front of the house enjoying the ending of the day. Much to our surprise, a caravan of camels and pack animals came down our street and stopped in front of our house. The men in the caravan were obviously of great wealth and importance. Thinking perhaps that they had lost their way, Joseph rose to meet them. I took the baby into the house. Joseph bowed respectfully and said, "Greetings, may I be of help to you?"

Three men slid from their camels and walked toward Joseph. They looked tired and dusty as if they had traveled a long distance. One of the men spoke. "Greetings, to you sir. We have come a long way in search of a king that was born in Bethlehem. We have seen his star and have followed it to this place. We have inquired of your King Herod. He told us of the prophecy:

"And you, O Bethlehem in the land of Judah,
are not least among the ruling cities of Judah,
for a ruler will come from you
who will be the shepherd for my people Israel
(Matthew 2:6 NLT)?

"Herod instructed us to come and find the newborn King of the Jews so that he could come and worship him. Last evening, we saw the star again, and it hovered over this house."

From my place behind the door, I heard Joseph invite the men inside. They entered the house quietly and reverently. When they saw Jesus in my arms, they were so overcome that they knelt down and worshipped him.

Unafraid, Jesus looked solemnly at these strange men in his house; then he laughed and clapped his hands!

Smiling, the men rose. One of them went outside and came back into the house followed by three servants bearing gifts. Each man presented a gift to Jesus. One man gave gold, the other gave frankincense, and the last gave him myrrh. We were overwhelmed by the value of these precious offerings.

After a short time, they reluctantly said that they must go. One of the men came over and knelt on one knee in front of me. Jesus was sitting on my lap. As a baby will do, Jesus reached out and touched his face. Smiling, the man took Jesus' little hand in his own and said, "Good-bye, my king. We will meet again."

The men and their entourage left soon after. With the babe asleep in my arms, Joseph and I sat for a while, staring and wondering at the beautiful gifts that the men had given Jesus.

*****

Several nights later, Joseph woke me up, urgently calling my name. "Mary, wake up! Wake up! Frightened and not knowing the cause of his concern, I instinctively reached for Jesus who was sleeping nearby in his little bed.

"What is the matter, Joseph?"

"We must leave. We must leave immediately. Jesus' life is in danger. An angel of the Lord appeared to me in a dream and said, '*Get up! Flee to Egypt with the child and his mother. Stay there until I tell you to return, because Herod is going to search for the child to kill him*'" (Matthew 2:13 NLT).

Not stopping to even question this dream, I started gathering the necessities for our journey. A short time later, we were packed and ready to leave. Joseph had gone to the stable and retrieved our little donkey. Putting the bags on him, we were soon on our way. Luckily, Jesus never woke up during this time.

We did not know until sometime later what had happened after we left. We had settled in a small town just over the Egyptian border. It was on the trade route from Galilee to Egypt. Joseph had quickly found work, as the town was growing and in great need of carpenters.

One evening, he came home and as was his usual habit, picked up Jesus. Instead of swinging him around until he squealed, Joseph held him close, not saying a word. Concerned, I asked, "Joseph, what is wrong?"

"Mary, I have heard terrible news."

Alarmed, I asked again, "What is it, Joseph?"

Jesus began to squirm in his arms, so Joseph gently put him down to play.

"A caravan came through town today. I was at the well, taking a break when I heard two of the travelers talking. From their conversation, I knew they had traveled from Jerusalem. I introduced myself and began asking questions about what was going on in Jerusalem and Judea. They said that Herod was still alive but seemed to be losing his sanity. They explained that Herod had heard that a king had been born in Bethlehem. A caravan of wise men had come through town following some star looking for this newborn king. Herod told them to find the little king and report back to him so that he could come and worship the king.

Joseph stopped his story and looked at me. I reached out and put my hand on Joseph's arm. "Joseph?" Putting his hand on top of mine, he said, "Mary, for some reason the wise men did not go back and report to Herod after they left us. Perhaps God warned them as he did us. Herod was so angry with this, that he ordered the death of all male children from the age of two to birth.

I caught my breath in horror. "Oh, no, Joseph!" I felt fear grip me, making me sick to my stomach. "No, Joseph, no!" Joseph wrapped his arms around me and held me tightly against him as I cried. I cried for all those mothers who mourned the death of their precious babies. I cried in fear for the evil that caused this awful thing to happen. I cried in relief that we had escaped this terrible holocaust.

Hearing my cries, Jesus waddled over and stood by our side. Sensing that his mother was upset, he patted my leg with his little hand. Looking down and seeing him standing there beside me, I pulled myself from Joseph's arms and reached down to pick him up. Holding him now between us, we realized, even more, the sweet privilege of having this child in our lives.

It was over a year later that we were able to return to Judea. One morning, Joseph shook me. "Mary, wake up." I opened my eyes to see him pacing around the room, already dressed.

"What is it, Joseph?" I asked sleepily.

With a huge smile on his face, Joseph sat down on the pallet beside me and gave me a quick kiss.

"Mary, we're going home."

"Are you sure?" I asked hopefully.

"Yes, God sent another angel to speak with me last night. He said, *'Arise, take the young child and His mother, and go to the land of Israel, for those who sought the young child's life are dead"* (Matthew 2:20).

We packed our belongings and left the next day. Home, we were going home! I was so anxious to see my family. How sweet it would be to put Jesus in my mother's arms and see her smile. Also, I was pregnant again and could not wait to share the news of the new baby with my family.

We were not sure where God would have us settle. It did not take long for God to give us an answer. We heard from travelers along the way that Archelaus was reigning over Judea instead of his father, Herod, so we were afraid to go into Judea. God warned Joseph one more time in a dream, and we turned aside into the region of Galilee. God guided us home! We were back in Nazareth with our family and friends. Our Jesus would be raised a Nazarene.

"Jesus grew in wisdom and in stature and in favor with God and all the people" (Luke 2:40. NLT).

James, the Brother of Jesus

Chapter Two

T he village was in mourning. The wailing echoed from the hills and drifted through the village, floating from house to house, touching each person's heart with sadness. The people of the village had lost a kind and true friend. He built their houses, cribs for their babies, and mangers for their animals. He was the one who lovingly crafted the beautiful trellises for their weddings and yes, even coffins for their funerals.

He was a good man. His name was Joseph, and he was my father. My name is James. I was only ten years old when my father died.

I was angry. I wanted my father back. I wanted to be able to sit on his lap and feel his arms around me as he whittled out the nails that he would need for the next day; to smell the rich, earthy fragrance of that newly cut wood.

I remember feeling so alone and left out. The mourners came; their moaning and wailing sent chills down my spine. I was furious with those ridiculous women; I just wanted them to go away. Friends and family surrounded my mother, so she was also lost to me during this time, encased in her own grief.

The only person I could turn to was my older

brother, Jesus. He was twenty, ten years older than me. He was the best big brother that a boy could have, patient with my pestering when my other brothers and sisters had no time for me. He listened to my non-stop conversation, even asking me questions at times.

I used to love to follow my father and Jesus as they went about their carpentry work in the village. They began teaching me the craft as soon as I was old enough to pick up a hammer. My job was to stand between the two of them and hold the board in place as they hammered. I enjoyed listening to them tell stories and laugh. Those two had a relationship that was based on mutual respect, humor, and love. My father was a master storyteller. His stories would have Jesus laughing so hard that nails would come spitting out of his mouth. Finally, Father would have to say, "James, Jesus, let's sit down for a while to rest."

So, on that terrible day, I went looking for my brother. I knew where to find him. He had a special place that he liked to go to when he wanted to be alone. It was on a hill overlooking Nazareth. My mother said she used to go there often when she was a young girl. She even told us that an angel had visited her on that same hill years ago.

I found Jesus sitting on a rock staring out over the valley. I didn't say a word but walked over and sat down next to him. He put his arm around my shoulder, and we sat like that not saying anything, not needing to speak.

It was so peaceful up there on that hill far away from the wailing of the mourners and the busyness of all the funeral preparations. The day had finally begun to cool down as a breeze blew softly from the north.

Finally, breaking the silence, I asked, "Jesus, where

is Abba? Where is he now? Why did he have to die? Why did God take him from us?" It seemed that when the questions finally began to spill out, I couldn't stop.

Jesus listened patiently, his arm still around me. I leaned closer to him as he began to speak. "James, as I sat here and prayed, I remembered Psalm 102.

'He has cut me down in midlife,
shortening my days.
But I cried to him, 'My God, who lives forever,
don't take my life while I am still so young!
In ages past, you laid the foundation of the earth,
and the heavens are the work of your hands.
Even they will perish, but you remain forever;
they will wear out like old clothing.
You will change them like a garment,
and they will fade away.
But you are always the same;
your years never end.
The children of your people
will live in security.
Their children's children
will thrive in your presence'
(Psalms 102:23-28 NLT).

"James, we may feel alone right now, but God has not rejected or forsaken us. God is with Joseph, our father, and He is with us. *We must draw close to our God, and He will draw close to us*" (James 4:8).

I wasn't sure I understood or was ready to hear what Jesus had to say, but I believed it because he said it. We sat there for a long time gazing down into the valley until the sun began to fade, and we knew that we had to return to our mother.

*****

The years after that passed quickly. Jesus stepped easily into the role of provider for our family. He had always been wise and mature beyond his years, and the entire family leaned heavily upon him. He was like a father to us. He taught me so much, not only about the craft of carpentry but also about life. He was good-natured, friendly, and always drew a crowd of friends. People enjoyed having him come to their homes to work because of the stories that he could tell. Our tiny carpentry shop was a gathering place for the village. Life was not easy for us in Galilee, but it was good.

And then it changed forever. I will never forget that day, the day Jesus left us. I had noticed that he had become quieter lately, often spending more and more time on the hill overlooking Nazareth. Mother sent me there to find him, to call him home for the evening meal. He was sitting on a boulder, motionless, head bowed, silhouetted by the hazy golden hues of the sun setting in the western sky. He knew immediately that I was there. I walked over and sat down beside him.

"James, I am leaving."

Stunned, I asked, "What do you mean?"

Looking intently at me, he said, "Do you remember the story of the time when I was twelve years old and stayed behind in the temple at Jerusalem?"

I nodded. I had heard the story many times. "Mother said that she was frantic with worry about you."

"Yes, she and Father searched for three days, almost giving up hope of ever finding me," he said. "But when they did find me, I asked my mother why they needed to search. I thought they would know that I would be in my Father's house."

I looked out toward the valley, remembering the story. "Mother said that they did not understand what you meant that day. She was just so glad to have found you."

"My Father is calling to me now, James. I hear His voice and I must go to him."

I shook my head. "You can't leave, Jesus. We need you here. The family needs you. Mother needs you . . . I need you."

"James, I know that you do not understand right now, but someday you will."

I stood up, angry, and hurt. "What is wrong with you? Are you out of your mind? A person does not leave his family and go off in search of . . . of . . ." I was so angry at this point that I could not even speak.

Quietly, Jesus finished my sentence. "My Father, James, I search for my Father."

"No! Your father is my father—Joseph of Nazareth. He is dead, Jesus. He died ten years ago. You are the father of this house now."

I ignored the pain that was evident on his face and continued my tirade. "Jesus, be reasonable. Please think some more about this . . . this spiritual quest." Then I said the one thing that I knew would hurt him the most. "You will break our mother's heart if you leave us."

"James, I have no choice."

At that point, Jesus stood up and embraced me. "My brother, you must be strong." He then turned and walked down the hill toward town.

I didn't follow him but stayed on that hill until it was almost too dark to see my way home. When I finally made my way back to our house, my mother was sitting on her bench outside the door. "Mother, he is gone."

"Yes, I know, James. He left an hour ago. He goes in search of your cousin John and . . ." Her voice trailed off.

I shook my head and said bitterly, "I know, Mother. He said he seeks his Father."

My mother reached for my hand.

*****

We did not see or hear from Jesus for several months. Somehow, I fell into a routine with my brothers Joseph, Simon, and Judas, going about our carpentry work, trying not to think about him, but missing him very much. We continued to hear word of our cousin John, dressed in camel's hair clothing, going about preaching repentance and baptizing people. We honestly didn't know what to make of this. Some people even called John a prophet of God. I thought he was probably crazy, stirring up people like that. More than one so-called prophet had been beheaded or crucified.

Jesus Turns Water Into Wine. (John 2:1-12)

The next time we saw Jesus was at the wedding of our cousin, Rachel. Rachel was a favorite cousin of mine, so my mother requested that I accompany her to the wedding. Joseph and Simon decided to go, also, and we were all looking forward to the weeklong festivities. Jesus arrived in Cana in the company of five strange men. My mother's eyes lit up when she saw him.

"My son, you are looking too thin."

He embraced her and smiled. " I am in good health,

Mother, I promise."

"Where have you been?" she asked.

"I have been in the Judean wilderness for a while."

She shook her head and hugged him one more time.

He turned toward me and gave me a brotherly bear hug. "James, are you taking good care of our mother?"

"Yes, she is well, Jesus."

Jesus introduced us to the five men.

"Mother, James, these are my friends, Andrew, John, Philip, Nathaniel, and Peter. They are my disciples." Jesus explained that he had met them by the Sea of Galilee after returning from the Judean wilderness.

> *And Nathanael Said To Him, "Can Anything*
> *Good Come Out Of Nazareth?"*
> *Philip said to him, "Come and see"* (John 1:46).

Andrew, Philip, Peter, and John were huge, brawny, fishermen; not what you would consider when you think of a disciple. I wasn't sure where Nathanael came from, but the men enjoyed joking with him about hanging around four fishermen and a Nazarene. The men were good-natured and seemed to enjoy being with Jesus. They were having a great time at the wedding.

It was good to be with Jesus, but strange also to see him out of the carpenter shop and in this role as a teacher. I wasn't sure I liked that role or what was happening to him.

After the wedding, Jesus asked us if we would like to accompany him and the disciples to Capernaum. My brothers and I did not want to go, but we knew that Mother did. (John 2:12)

"James, I do want to go and see where Jesus is staying, to see if he is taking care of himself."

I smiled at her fondly. Our mother will always be worried about us. We will always be children in her eyes.

Jesus was staying at the home of Peter's mother-in-law in Capernaum. It was a tiny house on the east shore of the Sea of Galilee. We spent two days along that beautiful sea, following and listening to Jesus, amazed at his teachings. We were told by the people in Capernaum that miracles happened when Jesus was around, but I saw none of that.

Later, after we were back home in Nazareth, Mother told me that something incredible had happened at the wedding in Cana. I remember that evening so well. We were sitting outside the house after supper, watching two of my nephews playing games in the street. We were laughing and joking with them, caught up in their joy.

All of a sudden, Mother turned toward me and said, "James, did you know that halfway through the wedding week, they ran out of wine?"

I looked at her and laughed. "Everyone was having a very good time."

She smiled. "Yes, and there were extra guests that came."

"Jesus' disciples?"

She nodded again. "Rachel came to me in tears halfway through the week and explained that they were running out of wine. She was very embarrassed."

"But Mother, the wine was excellent to the end. The wine at the end of the week was even better than the wine at the beginning. Usually, by that time the wine steward brings out the poorer quality wine."

"It was a miracle, James."

"Yes, it was a miracle that they had enough money to go out and buy such excellent wine."

"No, it was a real miracle."

"I don't understand, Mother."

"Jesus turned water into wine," she said softly.

"What did you say?" I asked incredulously.

"I found Jesus and explained the situation to him. At first, he was reluctant to even listen to me. But finally, he told the servants to get the six stone ceremonial pots and fill them with water. He told the servants to dip some out and take it to the master of the banquet."

"Yes, I remember the master of the banquet commenting on the excellent wine that was served after everyone was full."

"James, I'm telling you that it was a miracle."

"Mother, water does not turn into wine." I had a difficult time believing this story. There had to be a natural explanation. I could not believe that my brother could turn water into wine.

*****

Several months later my brother Joseph returned home from visiting Jerusalem for the Passover. He found me in the shop hammering a lattice together for an upcoming wedding.

"James, I have heard word of our brother, Jesus."

At the tone of his voice, I stopped what I was doing immediately.

"What have you heard?"

"Jesus was also in Jerusalem for the Passover. *In the temple area he saw merchants selling cattle, sheep, and doves for sacrifices; and he saw money changers behind their counters*" (John 2:13 NLT).

"Yes, it is a despicable practice; we have spoken of

it before."

"Well, this time Jesus did something about it."

"What do you mean, Brother?"

"Jesus made a whip from some ropes and chased them all out of the temple. He drove out the sheep and oxen, scattered the money changers' coins over the floor, and turned over their tables. Then, going over to the people who sold doves, he told them, 'Get these things out of here. Don't turn my Father's house into a marketplace!'" (John 2:15,16 NLT).

"Did they arrest him?"

"No, it is difficult to believe that they did not because he made some comment about destroying the temple and then raising it after three days."

Joseph shook his head. "What has happened to our brother, James?"

*****

It was the Sabbath, a day like many others. My brothers and I always looked forward to this day. We enjoyed our short walk to the synagogue, talking and laughing together about the happenings of the week. Our conversation often included Jesus and the extraordinary things that seemed to happen around him.

Laughing to myself, I said, "Remember the time the man pounded on our door looking for bread for breakfast? It was the middle of the night, and our father had to get up off of his pallet to answer the door. Father was never in a very good mood when awakened from his sleep like that. Before he could give the man a piece of his mind, Jesus appeared at the door, bread in hand. He quickly gave the man the bread and steered Father back to his bed. I never did know why the man needed bread in the middle of the night or where Jesus got that bread."

My brothers laughed and shook their heads. It seemed like Jesus was always in the right place at the right time. There was silence as we approached the synagogue. We all missed him so much.

We entered the synagogue, comfortable in the familiar place, nodding and smiling at friends. We sat down in our places and waited. Suddenly, I heard loud whispering at the back of the room; I turned around and saw Jesus walking down the aisle. He smiled at me and sat down.

When it was time to read the scripture for the day, the book that contained the prophetic words of Isaiah the prophet was reverently handed to Jesus. He opened the book and began to read:

"The Spirit of the Lord is upon Me,
Because He has anointed Me
To preach the gospel to the poor;
He has sent Me to heal the brokenhearted,
To proclaim liberty to the captives
And recovery of sight to the blind,
To set at liberty those who are oppressed;
To proclaim the acceptable year of the Lord"
(Luke 4:16-19).

Jesus then closed the book, gave it back to the attendant, and sat down. All eyes in the synagogue were upon him. There was a moment when the only sound that you could hear was the breathing, or in my case, the lack of breathing, of the thirty men in the room.

He said, *"Today this Scripture is fulfilled in your hearing"* (Luke 4:21).

There was a murmur throughout the room, and people began whispering.

"What gracious words."

"What does he mean?"

"*Is this not Joseph's son*" (Luke 4:22)?

Jesus stood up once again and faced the crowd. He replied, *"You will undoubtedly quote me this proverb: 'Physician, heal yourself'—meaning, 'Do miracles here in your hometown like those you did in Capernaum.' But I tell you the truth, no prophet is accepted in his own hometown* (Luke 4:23, 24 NLT).

"Certainly, there were many widows in Israel who needed help in Elijah's time when there was no rain for three and a half years and hunger stalked the land. Yet Elijah was not sent to any of them. He was sent instead to a widow of Zarephath—a foreigner in the land of Sidon. Or think of the prophet Elisha, who healed Naaman, a Syrian, rather than the many lepers in Israel who needed help" (Luke 4:25-27 NLT).

I felt my heart begin to race as I heard Jesus speak. I knew that those words would make the men in the synagogue very angry. The murmur began to get louder. Suddenly one voice, then another, began shouting:

"Who do you think you are, coming here and speaking such words?"

"How dare you accuse us of being like the unbelievers in the days of Elisha."

"Are you a gentile lover, Jesus?"

"You are just a carpenter. Go back to your bench."

"Do you compare yourself to Elijah?"

"He must have a demon."

The more they shouted the angrier they got until suddenly the entire group from the back of the synagogue rushed forward to where he was standing and grabbed hold of Jesus. My other brothers and I tried to hold them back, but we were no match for the size of the group. I could not believe this was happening.

The crowd grabbed Jesus and began pulling him out of the synagogue. They took him up to the hill on the edge of the city and were planning on pushing him over the cliff. In the mayhem, Joseph and I were able to make our way back to Jesus. I'm not sure to this day that I can explain what happened at that point. When we reached him and put our hands on him, we suddenly found ourselves on the edge of the crowd and able to slip our way to safety.

After making sure that he was finally out of harm's way, we stopped for a while along the road and rested. Joseph and I had no words for Jesus. We were in shock over what had just occurred at the synagogue, but Jesus seemed unfazed by it all.

"My brothers, I must leave you and meet up with my disciples in Capernaum."

I spoke sharply to him, "I do not understand what is happening to you."

His dark brown eyes studied me for a long moment.

"I know that James, but there will come a time someday when you will understand."

"Do you wish to die or be put in prison?" None of this made any sense to me.

"No, I do not want either one of those things to happen," Jesus answered softly. "I seek to do only my Father's will."

I knew that it was futile to continue this conversation. "We will leave you, my brother."

Joseph and I stood and embraced Jesus. A strange thing happened at that embrace. I felt an indescribable sense of well-being and power flow from Jesus into me. I would have fallen if he had not grabbed hold of my arm to steady me. I stepped back quickly, stunned by this sensation.

"Shalom, my brothers." Jesus turned and walked away.

*****

We returned to Nazareth to face the fear of our mother and the hostility of some of our neighbors. The town was buzzing about the scene at the synagogue. People were shaking their heads and wagging their tongues.

Mark 3:20-21

"Your brother has gone off the deep end, James," people would say.

"Who does he think he is, saying that he is the Messiah?"

"You need to go get him and bring him home where he belongs."

"He looks so thin."

"I heard that the crowds are so great now that he and his disciples do not even take time to eat."

Our mother listened to this prattle until she could take it no more.

One day she cornered me in the carpenter shop and said, "James, we must go and get Jesus. I am so frightened for him."

I knew that it was futile to argue with my mother. "I will find my brothers, and we will leave tomorrow at dawn."

Matthew 12: 46-50; Mark 3:31-33; Luke 8:19-21 (Nlt)

We arrived in Capernaum around noon and went directly to the home of Peter's mother-in-law. The crowd had indeed grown since the last time we were in Capernaum. People were everywhere. They were hanging out the windows, on top of the roof, and stuffed in the doorways.

"How are we to get to him, James?" Mother asked worriedly, as a man stepped in front of her and elbowed her out of the way.

Frustrated, I said to Simon, "I will see if I can send word by one of those fellows up there in the window. Perhaps they can tell Jesus that we are outside and want to speak to him."

I pushed my way through the crowd until I could get close enough to the window. I gave my message to a young man who was sitting on the ledge. Nodding at me, he turned toward the inside, and I heard him explain to Jesus that we wanted to speak to him. I could tell that Jesus was answering him.

Impatiently I said, "What is it, man? What does he say?"

"He said, *'Who is my mother? Who are my brothers? These are my mother and brothers. Anyone who does God's will is my brother and sister and mother'*"(Mark 3:33, 34 NLT).

Angry, I went back to my mother and brothers waiting at the edge of the crowd. Shaking my head and not wanting to tell my mother what Jesus said, I explained, "He cannot see us right now."

"We will wait here, then, until he comes out," my

mother said stubbornly.

Later that same day Jesus left the house and sat beside the lake. A large crowd soon gathered around him, so he got into a boat. Then he sat there and taught as the people stood on the shore (Matthew 13:1, 2 NLT).

Much to my mother's regret, we never did get to talk to Jesus that day, but we did decide to follow the crowd down to the shore of the Sea of Galilee. We listened as he told a story about a farmer who went out to plant seeds. As he scattered the seeds, some fell on the path, some fell on shallow soil, some fell among thorns, and some fell on fertile soil. The birds quickly ate the seeds on the path. The seeds thrown on the shallow soil germinated but soon died because they could not produce roots. The seeds that were planted in the thorns were choked out, but the seeds that fell on fertile soil produced a crop that was thirty, sixty, and even a hundred times as much as he had planted.

We spoke of the story on our way home from Capernaum.

"I am not sure what Jesus is teaching when he uses these stories," I said.

"Well, I have never read anything like that in the Torah," Joseph shrugged, dismissing the whole thing.

We returned once again to our homes and our work, trying not to think of our brother. This was difficult to do because people were constantly coming to us and telling tales about Jesus. Many times, they would just laugh and shake their heads.

"Did you hear that Jesus sent a herd of pigs over a cliff?" one neighbor told me, laughing so hard that he had to hold his side.

"That's nothing," another man said, "I heard that he raised a girl from the dead."

"I even heard that Jesus calmed a storm."

And so, the rumors continued. I tried to avoid people as much as possible.

The People Of Nazareth Would Not Believe.
(Matthew 13:53-58; Mark 6:1-6)

One morning I was working at my bench, trying to figure in my mind the best way to fit a table together. The table was to be crafted from a beautifully grained piece of olive wood. I knew what I wanted it to look like, but I had yet to create the perfect design. The Sabbath would begin at sundown. I wanted to have a good start before then, but I couldn't seem to concentrate. Finally, giving up, I sat down and stared at the wood in defeat.

"Unless the Lord builds the house, they labor in vain who build it" (Psalm 127:1).

I looked up to see Jesus standing at the door.

I smiled, remembering that our father would often quote that scripture to us as we began a new project.

"Greetings, Brother. What brings you to Nazareth?"

"I will be teaching in the synagogue tomorrow."

"But, Jesus, do you not remember what happened the last time you were here?" I asked in disbelief.

"Yes, I want to preach one more time; perhaps this time the people will believe in me."

The next morning, Simon and I accompanied Jesus to the synagogue. All was quiet this time as he got up to preach. Perhaps the people were embarrassed and regretted their actions from the last time. Even though they did not become violent, they still did not believe in him or what he said. The murmuring continued.

"Where did he get all his wisdom and the power to perform such miracles?"

"He's just the carpenter, the son of Mary and brother of James, Joseph, Judas, and Simon."

"Yes, his sisters live right here among us."

Jesus heard their murmuring as he left the synagogue.

As we were going down the steps of the synagogue, Jesus stopped and said to the crowd, *"A prophet is honored everywhere except in his own hometown and among his relatives and his own family"* (Mark 6:1-4 NLT).

★★★★★

"Now He Could Do No Mighty Work There, Except That He Laid His Hands On A Few Sick People And Healed Them" (Mark 6:5).

The people parted for him as he walked down the steps, shrugging their shoulders and turning their backs on him. At the bottom of the steps, Anna, an old family friend waited patiently. Her beautiful, wrinkled face broke into a toothless smile when she saw Jesus. Her back was bent with age causing her to have to twist crookedly to look up at him.

She spoke softly and said, "Jesus, it is good to see you." She then turned slowly toward Simon and me and smiled, speaking to us also. "Simon, James, it is good to see you as well."

Jesus looked at her expectantly, a look of concern on his face.

"Anna, what do you need from me?"

Anna looked at Simon and me hesitantly and then turned toward Jesus.

"May I speak to you alone, Jesus?"

He nodded, and they walked slowly arm in arm over to a beautiful, old olive tree. Anna sat down on a bench beneath the tree. I noticed that Jesus sat on the ground, propped up against the trunk so that Anna would not have to strain to look up at him. Curious, I watched from afar as Anna spoke to Jesus. I could tell that she was upset. He listened with rapt attention nodding now and then. At once, he stood up and put his hand on her shoulder. Fascinated, I watched as Anna slowly stood and then straightened up until she was looking at him directly, a huge smile on her face. She reached up to hug him, her small stature dwarfed by his. With a smile equal to Anna's, Jesus said something else to her. Anna nodded and backed away from Jesus. With a wave, she walked briskly away, her back as straight as someone half her age.

I turned toward Simon, not believing what I just saw. He was staring at Jesus and shaking his head.

"What happened, Brother?" he asked in disbelief.

"I'm not sure," I said truthfully.

Jesus walked back to where we were standing. He looked at both of us, a sad smile on his face. *"Brothers, I marvel at the unbelief that I see on your faces. Nazareth is not a good place for me right now, is it? Therefore, I will leave to meet up with my disciples. There's not much that I can accomplish here in Nazareth. I will send my disciples out to preach the good news elsewhere."* (Mark 6: 6, 7)

That was the last time that Jesus preached in Nazareth. We heard that John had been beheaded, and Jesus' life was now in even more danger. We lost patience with the obvious disregard that he had for his life and tried to put him out of our minds. Once again, rumors circulated around the village as people continued to wag their tongues. We tried to protect our mother from them but knew it was useless.

*****

Jesus still came to visit us, often stopping by at night after the village had settled into their homes. One cool, beautiful evening in October, we were all sitting around the table after a meal, talking with Jesus. Simon, Joseph, and I were leaving the next day to travel to Jerusalem for the Festival of Shelters.

Joseph, especially, had no patience with Jesus and often ridiculed him, much to the dismay of our mother.

Jesus' Brothers Ridicule Him. (John 7:1-9)

"Jesus," Joseph scoffed, "Come, go to Judea with us for the festival. You know that the Festival of Shelters is a family celebration. Besides, if you want people to see your miracles, Jerusalem is where you need to be. *You can't become famous if you hide like this! If you can do such wonderful things, show yourself to the world*" (John 7:4 NLT).

"Joseph, that is enough!" Mother said angrily.

Calmly, Jesus looked at Joseph and replied, "*Now is not the right time for me to go. But you can go anytime, and it will make no difference. The world can't hate you, but it does hate me because I accuse it of sin and evil. You go on. I am not yet ready to go to this festival, because my time has not yet come*" (John 7:6-8 NLT).

At that, Joseph stood up, shook his head, and walked out the door.

Early the next morning, we packed our belongings on our little donkey and left Nazareth for Jerusalem.

Jesus and Mother stood quietly and watched, bidding us a safe journey. Later, we learned that Jesus met up with his disciples and traveled to Jerusalem, though secretly, staying out of public view for a while.

When we arrived in Jerusalem, the streets were lined with shelters for the festival. We searched for several hours until we finally found an empty spot along a street that was fairly close to the temple. My brothers and I unloaded our donkey and began building our shelter.

"Do you need some help?" Two men called to us from their shelter close by. They walked up and introduced themselves. "My name is Demetrius, and this is my brother, Andrew. We live here in Jerusalem, so we were able to build our shelter yesterday for our families."

"Thank you, my friends," said Joseph. "We appreciate your help."

"Where are you from?" asked Demetrius.

"We come from Nazareth," explained Joseph.

John 7:11-13

Demetrius' face brightened, and he said, "Nazareth? Isn't that where the miracle worker, Jesus, comes from?"

Joseph ducked his head and looked toward me, warning me with his eyes not to say anything.

Slowly, I nodded my head. "Yes, we know of him."

Demetrius glanced around as if afraid someone was listening. He lowered his voice and whispered, "Andrew and I have seen him perform a miracle." Motioning for us to come closer, he said, "We saw him heal a blind man."

Seeing the incredulous look on my face, Andrew

joined in. "It's true. This man was blind from birth. We grew up with him."

"Just yesterday," Demetrius lowered his voice even more, "a group of Jewish leaders from the synagogue was asking us if we had seen or heard of Jesus at the festival. Everyone is whispering about him as we do now, but no one dares to speak favorably about him, because we are all afraid of getting into trouble with the Jewish leaders."

With Demetrius' and Andrew's help, it did not take us long to finish our shelter. We sat down to enjoy watching the people as they walked to and fro down the crowded, cobblestone street. Children were running around playing games and pranks. There were country people like us, wide-eyed at being in Jerusalem, porters carrying huge loads on their heads to the marketplace, and beggars hoping to profit from the pilgrims in Jerusalem for the festival. We saw soldiers, bored and hot in their Roman uniforms. Sadducees and Pharisees, pompous in their brocaded robes, walked hurriedly to the temple. Merchants hawked their wares from shelter to shelter, and women, their pots balanced on their heads, walked to the well to draw water. The street was teeming with people, noisy and raucous, causing me to yearn for the quiet hills of Nazareth.

By the next morning, most work activities had stopped. It was the fifth day after the Day of Atonement, and the Festival of Shelters had begun. Joseph and I awoke early to join the crowds as they made their way to Temple Square. The streets were lined with palm fronds, leafy branches, and willows. The first day of the festival always began with the sacred assembly at the temple and the presentation of our offerings to God. The high priest stood up to teach, reminding us of God's protection and guidance in the wilderness.

The next two days were the same; nights filled with dancing and singing, and days gathered in the sacred assembly, worshiping God. The Festival of Shelters was always one of our favorite festivals.

John 7:14-52 (NLT)

On the third day, we again joined the throng as they gathered in the temple. We had overslept that morning, not getting much sleep the night before, so we found ourselves at the back of the crowd. Joseph, Simon, and I tiptoed, trying the best that we could to see what was happening. All of a sudden there was a hush among the crowd. We had no idea what was going on until gradually word came back to us that Jesus of Nazareth was speaking.

Joseph looked at us and frowned. "Follow me; let's see if we can get up closer."

I grabbed hold of the back of Joseph's robe and followed his large bulk as he pushed his way through the crowd closer to the front. When we finally found a spot where we could hear what was going on, a Jewish leader beside us mumbled to himself, "How does he know so much when he hasn't studied everything we've studied?"

As if to answer him, Jesus said, *"I'm not teaching my ideas, but those of God who sent me. Anyone who wants to do the will of God will know whether my teaching is from God or is merely my own. Those who present their ideas are looking for praise for themselves, but those who seek to honor the one who sent them are good and genuine. None of you obeys the law of Moses. In fact, you are trying to kill me"* (John 7:16-19 NLT).

There was a stunned silence; then a man in the

crowd yelled, "You are demon-possessed! Who's trying to kill you?"

Calmly, Jesus answered. *"I did one miracle on the Sabbath, and you were amazed. But you work on the Sabbath, too, when you obey Moses' law of circumcision. For if the correct time for circumcising your son falls on the Sabbath, you go ahead and do it so as not to break the law of Moses. So why should you be angry with me for healing a man on the Sabbath? Look beneath the surface so you can judge correctly"* (John 7:21, 24 NLT).

There were nods of affirmation throughout the crowd. People all around us began talking to each other.

"Isn't this the man they are trying to kill?"

"Yes, but here he is, speaking in public, and they say nothing to him."

A man beside Joseph turned to him and said, "Can it be that our leaders know that he really is the Messiah?"

I looked over at Joseph as he snapped back at the man, "But how could he be? We know where this man comes from. When the Messiah comes, he will simply appear; no one will know where he comes from."

Joseph then threw up his hands in disgust, turned around, and said, "James, let's get out of here."

As if hearing these remarks, Jesus spoke out as we turned and left. *"Yes, you know me, and you know where I come from. But I represent one you don't know, and he is true. I know him because I have come from him, and he sent me to you."*

We threaded our way back through the crowd to our shelter. Our new friends, Demetrius and Andrew joined us soon after. They were thrilled yet amazed that Jesus had stood up and preached at the temple that morning.

"Did you hear him? Were you there?" asked Demetrius.

Joseph scowled. "Yes, we were there. We heard him."

"Did you know that the leaders of the synagogue wanted him arrested?" asked Andrew. "They sent out the temple guards, but for some reason, they did not lay a hand on him."

Demetrius interrupted, "When they came to arrest him, Jesus said, *'I will be here a little longer. Then I will return to the one who sent me. You will search for me but not find me. And you won't be able to come where I am.'*"

"What did he mean by that?" snapped Joseph.

"Well, not even the Jewish leaders could figure that one out. They thought maybe he was going to leave the country and go to the Jews in other lands or to the gentiles."

Andrew chimed in again. "I think they need to leave him alone. Would you expect the Messiah to do more miraculous signs than this man has done?"

Joseph shrugged, dismissing all of this with a wave of his hand. He sat down heavily on his pallet, crossed his arms, and retreated into one of his infamous bad moods.

On the last day of the festival, Joseph revived from his bad mood and asked me if I would go with him to the market to purchase fruit for our meal that day.

A crowd had gathered, milling around and talking excitedly to each other. I knew immediately that Jesus must be there. People were shouting questions at him, some of them angry.

Jesus shouted back, *"Let anyone who is thirsty come to me and drink. Whoever believes in me, as Scripture has said, rivers of living water will flow from within them"* (John

7:37, 38).

"What is he talking about now?" mumbled Joseph.

Turning toward him, a man beside Joseph said, "*He is the Messiah!*" (John 7:41 NLT)

Another man looked at Joseph and me and our clothes, knowing that we were from the area of Galilee, shook his head and scoffed, "*How can the Messiah come from Galilee? Does not Scripture say that the Messiah will come from David's descendants and from Bethlehem, the town where David lived?*" (John 7:42 NLT)

Of course, Joseph and I knew full well that Jesus had indeed been born in Bethlehem. Our mother had told us the story of the trip from Nazareth to Galilee many times. We knew that Jesus had been born in a stable and that something miraculous had happened when Jesus was born, but our mother never did tell us all of the details.

Before Joseph could reply to the man with one of his famous retorts, we were pushed aside by a group of the temple guards, obviously sent again to try and arrest Jesus. Remarkably, they stopped short when they saw him and stood with the crowd and listened. Unfazed by their presence, Jesus continued to speak to the crowds.

Joseph and I did not stay long after that. We returned to our shelter and began to dismantle it. We left at dawn the next morning, the quietness broken only by the crowing of the roosters announcing the start of another day. I always experienced a letdown and even a sense of sadness at the end of a festival; this morning I felt especially bereft as we made our way through the empty streets of Jerusalem.

Thank goodness, Joseph did not choose to speak, so I was left with my own quiet, yet jumbled thoughts. I recalled the words that I heard Jesus say, *"Yes, you both know me, and you know where I am from; and I have not come of Myself, but He who sent Me is true, whom you do not know. But I know Him, for I am from Him, and He sent Me"* (John 7:28, 29 NKJV).

Something rang true, deep within my heart, when I heard Jesus say that. But it was all so very confusing. Jesus was my brother, and I thought I knew him as well as I knew myself. This man had become a stranger to me.

That was the last time that Joseph and I heard Jesus preach. It was said that after the Festival of Shelters, he preached in various towns in Judea, returned to Jerusalem for a time, and then left again and traveled to the region east of the Jordan. Of course, travelers brought us word telling of the miraculous events that surrounded the miracle worker, Jesus of Nazareth.

Back in Nazareth, I felt strangely restless and unsettled. The winter was uneventful, passing quickly into spring. Soon it was time for the Passover celebration. One morning I was at my bench when I heard a soft knock on the door.

"Come in."

"Good morning, my son."

My mother was standing in the door, silhouetted by the early morning light. It reflected the inner light that always seemed to shine from within her. She was beautiful. But, of course, she was my mother and very special to me. I squinted my eyes to look at her. She smiled.

"James, I am leaving with my sister and her husband to go to Jerusalem for the Passover."

I felt an uneasiness in my spirit as I heard her say this; I felt a strange foreboding. "Do you want me to go with you, Mother?" I asked. "Will Joseph or Simon be going?"

"No, you must all stay here."

I looked at her, wondering why she wanted to go to Jerusalem at this particular time, and why she did not want us to go with her.

Sensing my confusion, she smiled sadly and said, "James, I must go, but I will be home soon."

As I hugged her good-bye, I knew instinctively that she hoped that Jesus would be at the Passover. Mother knew how we felt about him, and she did not want to deal with Joseph's ridicule or my questions. Jesus was her oldest son, and she was worried about him.

Joseph and I helped her finish packing her little donkey. Gruffly, Joseph said, "If you run into our brother, tell him to come home." He hesitated and then mumbled, "Tell him that we miss him."

Mother smiled and said, "Joseph, I will tell him that."

We got word of the crucifixion two weeks later. It's interesting how an ordinary day can be turned into one that stands out for all time—for all eternity.

A messenger was sent to tell my brothers and sisters the news. Jesus had been crucified; he was dead—but then he told us that there was a rumor that he was alive. Rumors were spreading throughout Jerusalem that Jesus had been raised from the dead.

We hovered together in our mother's house, our children, wives, husbands—whispering, questioning, wondering. What did this all mean? What had happened?

We worried about our mother. She went to Jerusalem to be with him. Was she in danger? What were we thinking, sending her off to Jerusalem to face this?

Always the impetuous one, Joseph said, "We will go to Jerusalem and find her."

Simon, Judas, and Joseph packed quickly to leave. It was decided that I was to stay in Nazareth to . . . to do what? To wait? To work? How does one move through the days after something like this has happened?

I couldn't eat; food felt like rocks in my stomach. When I lay on my pallet to try and sleep, my mind raced and jumped, thinking about and remembering my brother. I was angry with him, angry that he had put himself in the position to be crucified. I cried, trying to muffle my sobs, but then screamed out at God. I was desperate to hear about what had happened.

On the fourth night, I finally fell into a fitful sleep. I woke early the next morning, bathed in sweat, needing to seek a breath of cool air. I decided to walk to the hill overlooking Nazareth, the hill where so much had happened. Perhaps I would find some comfort there.

He was seen by Peter and then by the Twelve. After that, he was seen by more than 500 of his followers. at one time, most of whom are still alive, though some have died. Then he was seen by James and later by all the apostles (1 Corinthians 15:6-8 NLT).

My numbed mind refused to even think as I made my way up that familiar hill. The beauty of the morning was lost to me. I tripped once, falling to my knees, numb even to that pain. I stayed there for a moment, catching my breath, and then stumbled back up and continued walking. Finally, at the top, I sat down heavily on the same boulder that Jesus and I had sat on so many times before. The sun was just peeking out of the horizon, dusting the valley with a soft, golden light. I stared at the sun, hardly blinking, my thoughts as motionless as my eyes.

Suddenly, as I gazed toward the rising sun, out of the rays of light, I saw an apparition walking toward me. Slowly blinking my eyes, I tried to make sense out of what I was seeing. I couldn't move; I was frozen. Could it be? No, this was impossible.

And then his voice said, "James."

I slowly stood up, stunned and bewildered.

Shaking my head and mouthing his name, I asked, "Jesus?"

"Yes, my brother, I am alive."

I looked at him again, still not believing my eyes. "You're alive! Jesus, how can this be?"

He walked toward me, smiling, his arms outstretched.

With a loud shout that echoed throughout the valley, I ran to my brother, grabbed hold of him, and hugged him.

"You're alive! You're alive!" Still holding on to him, I backed away at arm's length and looked at his beloved face. Laughing at me, he said, "Yes, little brother, I am very much alive." With a whoop, I ran to the edge of the cliff, threw back my head, and shouted out to the valley below, "He's alive! He's alive!"

Suddenly, I knew. It all made sense now. I fell to my knees and cried out, "Lord Jesus." Tears were streaming down my face as the truth flooded over me. Jesus—my brother, Jesus is the Messiah.

Jesus walked over and put His hand on my shoulder. "Rise my brother, we must talk. I have plans for you."

We sat once again on that rock overlooking the valley and talked of many things. There was so much to be said. Jesus looked at me and said, "Brother, none of this is going to be easy, *but whenever trouble comes your way, let it be an opportunity for joy. For when your faith is tested, your endurance has a chance to grow. So, let it grow, for when your endurance is fully developed, you will be strong in character and ready for anything*" (James 1:2-4 NLT).

My heart burned within me as we talked. There was so much that I needed to know. Where should I begin? What was I to do?

"James, you must meet up with Simon and the other disciples. You will be welcomed among them. They have already embraced our mother. I have told them to wait in Jerusalem until the Father sends you what He promised. *John baptized with water, but in just a few days you will be baptized with the Holy Spirit*" (Acts 1:5 NLT).

I hesitated before speaking, "What of our other brothers? What of Joseph?"

Jesus smiled, thinking of our outspoken brother. He then actually laughed out loud and said, "Joseph will be one of my most faithful followers."

We sat together, facing God's glorious sunset. I then turned and looked one more time into His precious face, my brother's face ... no, the face of my God.

He smiled. "Shalom, James. We will meet again." And then He was gone.

Interlude One

Before Abraham Was, I Am

John 1; John 8:58

Before Abraham was, *I AM*
The Word
made flesh
that
came into
the world.

Before Abraham was, *I AM*
The Light
that
shines in
the darkness.

Before Abraham was, *I AM*
The Son of Man
who gave you the
right
to be called
the children of God.

The Baptist

Chapter Three

Luke 3

Now in the fifteenth year of the reign of Tiberius Caesar, Pontius Pilate being governor of Judea, Herod being tetrarch of Galilee, his brother Philip tetrarch of Iturea and the region of Trachonitis, and Lysanias tetrarch of Abilene, while Annas and Caiaphas were high priests, the word of God came to John the son of Zacharias as in the wilderness (Luke 3:1-3).

My name is John. I am thirty years old and have lived in the desert for most of my life. My father, Zacharias, took me there when I was thirteen. I still remember that day. It happened soon after my Bar Mitzvah, the day I became a man in the eyes of God. At the time, I did not realize that I was to leave my family forever.

I had been told many times by my mother the circumstances of my unusual birth. Even when I was a small child, my mother would explain that God had a special plan for me. I truly did not understand. But the day had arrived, and I was going to have to leave my beloved mother and father and go live among the Wise Fathers.

As the only child of Elizabeth and Zacharias, I admit to being a bit spoiled and very strong-willed. My parents doted on me. My father took me to the temple as soon as I was old enough to understand the importance of sitting still so that I could listen and watch the priests as they went about their duties. I was always fascinated by it all. My father told me that as a son of Aaron, I must take on the priestly duties someday, also.

Although I was an only child, I was surrounded by a large extended family. There were aunts, uncles, and dozens of cousins. I was especially close to Mary's son, Jesus. Being only five months apart in age, he was a part of my story, and I was a part of his.

Jesus attended my Bar Mitzvah, along with Mary, Joseph, and Jesus' other brothers and sisters. These occasions were always joyous in the lives of Jewish families. I noticed my mother and Mary talking at length, proudly watching Jesus and me closely.

After the celebration, Jesus and his family would leave to go back to Nazareth. Before he left, he ran up to me and said, "John, I will see you soon in Jerusalem." When he said Jerusalem, his face lit up with pleasure and excitement. We both loved these annual trips to Jerusalem for the Passover. It was very exciting for two young boys to be in such a city. All of the sights, sounds, and even smells of the sacred city always thrilled us. We grasped each other's arms and promised to see each other very soon. I did not realize at the time how quickly my life would change after that.

*****

Three months later, I accompanied my mother and father to Jerusalem. I was anxious to meet up with Jesus and his family. My father had the honor of serving at the temple this year. We were to go a few days early so that he could prepare. It was his duty to keep the incense burning on the altar of the Most Holy Place. Remarkably, the last time he had the privilege of doing this was twelve years ago when an angel came and told him that I was going to be born. At least that was the story that my mother told me.

I met up with Jesus several days later. We were camping outside the Western Wall of Jerusalem. "John!" I heard my name and knew that it could only be Jesus. We embraced as brothers, both of us talking at once.

"Come, Cousin," Jesus said. "We have much to see and so little time."

We each went to tell our parents where we were going, and then we raced toward the West Gate. The streets were already crowded with pilgrims. There were vendors and merchants, soldiers, and performers. We walked through the narrow streets, wide-eyed and excited.

"We must go to the temple," Jesus said suddenly.

"Yes," I answered. "We might see Father there."

We made our way through the crowd, weaving in and out as only small boys can do. We stopped short when we arrived at the Temple Square. God's temple never failed to take my breath away as I looked up at the shining white marble buildings. They glistened like diamonds in the bright, eastern sunlight.

For once, Jesus was speechless. He walked toward the front entrance of the temple reverently. I was so busy looking around that I didn't realize that he was about to enter a part of the temple that was forbidden to us.

"Jesus." I called. "Where are you going? Jesus, wait!"

He finally stopped and turned around toward the

sound of my voice. I ran up to him and asked him one more time, "Where were you going? You know we can't go in there."

He shook his head as if trying to wake himself up. He looked around one more time. "John, this is my Father's house. I heard him call to me."

We sat down together on the marble steps. I remember the feel of the warm, smooth marble beneath my hand, the sound of the shofar calling men to worship, and the things that we said to each other. I will always remember that day because it was one of the last times we were together for many years.

After a while, we walked slowly back to our camp, parting with a promise to see each other soon. Jesus was leaving with his family at dawn the next day. My family was to stay around Jerusalem for a few more days, waiting for my father to finish his duties.

I spent the next day pleasantly enough. My mother was not feeling well, so I helped her around the camp. I went to bed early that night but was awakened in the early hours the next morning.

"John, wake up." I opened my eyes to see my father shaking me. "Mary and Joseph are here looking for Jesus. Did you happen to see him yesterday?"

Trying to make sense out of what I heard, I struggled to sit up on my pallet. "Father, what did you say? What is wrong?"

"Jesus is missing, John. Have you seen him?"

"No. We were together two days ago, but he left with his family early yesterday morning."

"Mary and Joseph thought he left with them, too," Father explained worriedly. "But last night when they stopped to make camp, he was nowhere to be found.

They had assumed that he was traveling with some other family members."

We all began searching as soon as it was light. There were still thousands of pilgrims in Jerusalem. Jesus and I had been all over that city. I thought carefully about where he might be. I spent one day walking the wall that surrounded the city, scanning the throngs of people. Mary and Joseph searched the marketplace. We gathered together that evening tired and discouraged but set out again the next day determined to find him. This went on for two more days.

On the morning of the third day, we were all sitting outside our tents. Mary and Joseph were exhausted by fear and worry. My father and mother had no more words of hope to give them. Breaking the silence, I asked if anyone had searched the temple area. My father looked at me. "I was there yesterday," he said, "but I did not see him."

"Jesus and I were there for a while on the day before he left Jerusalem." Remembering back on that day, I told them how I had to stop him before he went into the forbidden area.

Looking intently at me, Mary said softly, almost to herself, "The temple, of course, the temple."

We all stood up at once. I followed Mary and Joseph as they made their way to the temple area. As we approached the outer courts, we saw a group of the Sanhedrin gathered together in a circle. It was their custom during the Passover to meet in the temple to discuss religious and theological questions. Walking closer, we saw Jesus. He was sitting in the middle of the group of men, listening and asking questions. We stood there, watching in amazement for a few minutes. One of the teachers had asked Jesus a question. We could not hear his reply, but the expressions on the teachers' faces showed that they were astonished by his answer.

Mary could stand it no longer. Relief and anger overcame her. It was written all over her face. How could he do this to her? The group was beginning to break up when she and Joseph walked over to Jesus.

"Son, why have you done this to us? Look, your father and I have sought You anxiously."

Jesus stood up and said in a respectful, yet questioning voice, *"Why do you seek me, Mother? Did you not know that I must be about My Father's business?"* (Luke 2:48, 49).

Mary glanced from Jesus to Joseph. Her proud, strong husband was looking at Jesus with tears in his eyes. She grabbed his hands, and they both reached out to Jesus to hug him.

I was truly confused by all of this. I told Jesus, Mary, and Joseph good-bye one more time and walked slowly back to tell my mother and father the good news. My parents were relieved and thankful that Jesus was found.

The next day, my father called me into the tent. In a subdued voice, my father said to me, "Son, your mother and I would like to speak to you."

Sensing the serious tone in his voice, I said, "Yes, Father, I am listening."

"Your mother and I have told you several times about the circumstances of your birth," my father said. "God blessed us by giving you to us in our old age. We have a responsibility to God to take good care of you. Because we are not young, we must make arrangements for you to be taken care of in case something happens to us. After these last three days, we are even more sure of this."

My father paused as if hesitant to continue. Confused and bewildered, I looked over at my mother. Her sweet face was turned away from me, but I could detect that she was crying.

"What are you saying to me?" I asked fearfully.

"We are sending you to live with the Wise Fathers," he said as he put his hand on my shoulder. "Your mother and I are old and not well. We must protect you from those who might harm you physically as well as spiritually. Before you were born, God sent an angel who instructed me that you should drink neither wine nor strong drink. From the time you were in your mother's womb, you were filled with the Holy Spirit. John, you will turn many of the children of Israel to the Lord their God. The angel also said *you will go before Him in the spirit and power of Elijah, to turn the hearts of the fathers to the children, and the disobedient to the wisdom of the just, to make ready a people prepared for the Lord*" (Luke 1:15-17).

My young mind could not grasp all that my father had spoken. I was only thirteen, and I did not want to leave the love and security of my parent's home. But the Spirit of God was within me—I have always felt him. I knew that what my father said was true.

Two months later, I tearfully hugged my mother good-bye and traveled to Qumran with my father. At the time we parted, I did not realize that I would never see my mother and father again. They both died soon after that.

✳✳✳✳✳

I grew into a man under the guidance of the strong, dedicated men of the Qumran community. I learned to be content with what I had, focusing inward on the Holy Spirit within me. He was my teacher and my friend.

One day I heard two of the scribes in the community discussing a particular verse from the book of Malachi that they had been copying that day.

"Behold, I send My messenger,
And he will prepare the way before Me.
And the Lord, whom you seek,
Will suddenly come to His temple,
Even the Messenger of the covenant,
In whom you delight.
Behold, He is coming,"
Says the Lord of hosts (Malachi 3:1).

Hearing this scripture, I felt the urging of the Holy Spirit within me to complete my life's journey. I was led out into the wilderness to spend time with my God. Taking nothing with me, I subsisted on locusts and wild honey. I even had to replace my clothes with a camel's hair vest, tied with a leather belt around my waist.

God spoke to my spirit in the wilderness. It was time. The Messiah was coming. I was chosen to prepare the way for him. Repent, repent . . . that was the word that came to me from God. I came out of the wilderness preaching repentance and baptizing God's people.

Matthew 3: 2-12; Luke 3:7-17

"Repent, for the kingdom of heaven is at hand."

People from Jerusalem, Judea, and all the regions around the Jordan came out to hear God's message through me. It was a difficult message that I preached, not easy to hear or accept. My words were especially harsh to one group of Pharisees and Sadducees who came out to listen. They stood apart from the others, challenging and arrogant in their pompous religiosity.

I spoke to them harshly. *"You brood of vipers! Who warned you to flee from the wrath to come?"* Their faces turned crimson as they raised their noses high in the air. I continued relentlessly. *"Bear fruits worthy of repentance. You think you are special because Abraham is your father? Don't you know that God can raise up children from these very stones at my feet?"*

"Even now the ax is laid to the root of the trees. Therefore, every tree which does not bear good fruit is cut down and thrown into the fire!"

They did not stay long after that, but retreated, dismissing me as a fraud and a fanatic. After they left, I turned toward the crowd, and with a softer voice said, *"I indeed baptize you with water unto repentance, but He who is coming after me is mightier than I, whose sandals I am not worthy to carry. He will baptize you with the Holy Spirit and fire."*

"His winnowing fan is in His hand, and He will thoroughly clean out His threshing floor and gather His wheat into the barn, but He will burn up the chaff with unquenchable fire."

Day after day people came. I searched each face in the crowd wondering who would be the One, and when He would come forth. So far, all I had seen were hundreds of people hungering for forgiveness and God. There was truly a spirit of repentance over the land.

People would ask, *"What shall we do?"*

I would reply, *"He who has two tunics, let him give to him who has none; and he who has food, let him do likewise."*

There were even tax collectors who came to be baptized, looking to me for hope and forgiveness. *"Teacher, what shall we do?"* These despised and hated men came forward in shame looking for the forgiveness that only can come from God, certainly not from man.

"Collect no more than what is appointed for you," I replied.

I noticed a group of soldiers edging closer to the crowd. Their faces were hard, chiseled by years of violence. They lived their brutal lives far from their homes and families.

"And what shall we do?" they asked.

"Do not intimidate anyone or accuse falsely and be content with your wages."

A group of Levites came out from Jerusalem to speak with me. The priests knew that I was the son of Zacharias and heir to the Levitical priesthood.

They were sent from the Sanhedrin. It was their duty to interrogate me to see if I was a false prophet. They were curious as to why I was baptizing people and acting in such a strange way.

John 1:19-28

"Who are you?"

Knowing where this question was leading, I said, *"I am not the Christ."*

"What then? Are you Elijah?"

"I am not."

"Are you the Prophet?"

"No," I said.

One of the Levites asked in an exasperated tone, "Who are you? We are from the Sanhedrin. They require an answer from you. What do you say about yourself?"

I looked at the group. Their eyes and posture reflected the disbelief in their hearts and minds. *"As the prophet Isaiah said, 'I am the voice of one crying in the wilderness: Make straight the way of the Lord.'"*

A Pharisee stepped out in front of the group shaking his head and asking, *"Why then do you baptize if you are not the Christ, nor Elijah, nor the Prophet"* (John 1:25)?

I was silent for a moment, choosing my words carefully. I finally answered him by saying, *"I baptize with water, but there stands One among you whom you do not know. It is He who, coming after me, is preferred before me, whose sandal strap I am not worthy to untie."*

The next day I rose early with a feeling of anticipation in my spirit. I sat alone for a time beside the river. It was cool and still, the silence broken only now and then by the song of a bird or the plop of a frog jumping into the water. The scripture *"Oh, taste and see that the Lord is good"* came to mind. Dwelling on David's psalm. I sat content.

My disciple, Andrew, called out to me, "Master, people are waiting for you on the other side of the river."

"Thank you, Andrew. I am coming."

It looked like there would be quite a crowd today. The people stood along the riverbank, talking quietly with each other. I stood with my back to the river, preaching repentance, imploring the crowd to turn from their sinful ways. At the end of the sermon, a large group came forward asking to be baptized.

After all the people were baptized, I scanned the bank, looking to see if anyone else wanted to come forward. Most of the people had gathered in small groups, trying their best to dry their wet clothes, laughing, and talking quietly together. That's when I saw him. He was standing off by himself watching me.

I knew—I knew immediately.

He walked toward me smiling that same smile that I remembered from my childhood. "Greetings, Cousin." he said. "It has been a long time."

I stood there for a moment, stunned. The One I had been waiting for was standing here in front of me. Jesus —He was Jesus. Of course. The knowledge of this flooded over me as the Holy Spirit quickened my mind and heart.

We embraced as brothers. Stepping back, Jesus looked at me and said, "John, I am ready for you to baptize me."

Matthew 3:14-17

Confused, I replied, *"I need to be baptized by You, and are You coming to me?"*

"Yes, John. The time has come for God to begin His work in me. This baptism will allow us to fulfill all righteousness. Remember when we were children, and we spoke together of the things our families had told us about our births? Remember, also, that day at the temple when I walked toward the Holy of Holies, and you restrained me?"

I smiled at him, remembering all that had been.

"My cousin, God has shown me that it is time to fulfill my destiny. I need you to be a part of this because you are the one God sent to prepare the way for me."

The crowd had thinned by this time, leaving only Jesus, two of my disciples, and myself. I asked the disciples to remain on the bank. Jesus and I waded slowly into the river. The sun was hot, beating down on my head and reflecting off the water. The river was clear, and

I could see several fish darting away from our feet. We stopped when we got to the waist-deep water. Jesus' face was serene as he bowed his head and closed his eyes.

With my left hand, I grabbed hold of his arm. His muscles were rock hard from years of carpentry. With my right arm, I braced his back to lower him into the water. I did so slowly, immersing his head and body beneath the cool, clear water of the Jordan River.

As I lifted him, a wind began to blow across the water, whipping up little white caps. With water dripping from him, Jesus stood with his eyes still closed, his face turned up toward heaven. Then an amazing thing happened. God spoke to my spirit and said, *"John, upon whom you see the Spirit descending and remaining on Him, this is He who baptizes with the Holy Spirit"* (John 1:33).

It was then I saw the Holy Spirit descend from heaven in the form of a dove. It flew down to us, hovering over Jesus then lighting on his shoulder. He visibly braced himself, shivered, and turned his head as if hearing something. Then I heard it—a voice came from heaven saying, *"This is My beloved Son, in whom I am well pleased"* (Matthew 3:17).

Sheer joy welled up inside of me, combined with a feeling of exhilaration. At that instant, I knew that my part in God's plan had come to an end. Jesus must increase, but I must decrease (John 3:30). I felt the contentment of a job well done. God would take over from here.

I smiled at Jesus. He clapped my shoulder and smiled back. Arm in arm, we waded slowly out of the river and sat down on the bank.

"We part again, John. God is calling me to go out into the wilderness. I have much to learn. We will not meet again in this life. Have courage, my cousin—someday we will meet again in the Holy of Holies."

The Calling of Simon and Andrew

Chapter Four

John 1:29-43; Luke 5:1-11

I t was a warm, sun-drenched morning in early June. The rays hit the water and then bounced back and soaked into my back. Simon and I were mending a hole in the net, a boring but essential job. We were running late that morning and were further delayed because of the unexpected tear in the net. Fishing had been meager last night, but we decided to go out one more time before we gave up and called it a day.

We had talked about many things that morning. Simon laughed at something his mother-in-law had said, his huge laugh echoing across the lake. He was truly fond of her and loved to quote some of the outrageous remarks that she would say. Then our conversation died down, and my thoughts moved to a man that I had met several weeks earlier.

I had been intrigued by the prophet John and had followed him for a while, listening, and learning. One day another disciple and I were standing and talking with John when a man named Jesus walked by.

John said quietly, *"Behold the Lamb of God."*

He looked at us and then at Jesus as if to say, "Go

and follow him."

Hesitant at first, we left John and hurried to catch up with the teacher. Hearing us, he turned and asked, *"What do you seek?"*

"Rabbi, where are you staying? We would like to talk to you."

He smiled. *"Come and see."*

We stayed the entire day with him, listening, and asking questions. Convinced that this man might be the Messiah, I brought Simon to meet Jesus several days later. He looked straight at Simon and said, *"You are Simon the son of Jonah. You shall be called Cephas."* Simon was not quite sure what to make of the man. Flustered at what Jesus had said, Simon remarked, "Andrew, we must get back to our boat." Simon would not speak of him again after that.

Today I was back with Simon on the boat taking care of business. We finished repairing the last hole in the net and were finally ready to push away from the shore. Simon was right in the middle of telling me something else that his mother-in-law had said when all of a sudden, he stopped mid-sentence. I glanced up to see Simon staring off down the beach. The smile that had been on his face had disappeared and was replaced by a look that I had never seen before. I followed his gaze, curious as to what or who had caught Simon's attention.

Then I saw him. Strangely, I felt a sense of destiny, a knowing that something was about to happen in my life. My eyes were riveted on the figure walking toward us. This person looked so familiar. Where had I seen him before? As he walked closer, I knew. It was Jesus.

He walked up to us and stopped. Looking intently at Simon and then at me, he said, "Greetings, my friends.

May I use your boat? I need to get away from the shore so that I might speak to the people." As Simon invited him to come aboard, I noticed for the first time a group of people who had trailed him down the beach. He helped us gather the nets together, and we threw them into the boat and pushed out from the shore.

Simon and I propped up against the bow of the boat and listened as he began to speak, his rich, deep voice amplifying across the water. The words caught my simple fisherman's ear. The message was clear and easy to understand.

I lost track of time, immersed in the quiet sounds of water lapping softly against the sides of the boat and the soothing message of this man. When he finished speaking there was no applause; the people stood quietly, some turning away, some simply sitting down on the beach to wait.

Smiling, he turned to Simon and me. "I have kept you from your work too long, my friends. Let's go fishing. Launch the boat toward the deep area of the lake."

At first, Simon began to argue with him. "The best part of the morning for fishing has already passed, and we fished for a while last night and didn't have any luck at all." Finally, Simon looked toward me and shrugged as if to say, "Why not?"

Jesus helped us hoist the sail, and we were on our way.

A short time later, we dropped anchor close to several other boats that were fishing nearby. I helped Simon throw the nets over the rail and into the water. Simon then moved to the back of the boat to wait while Jesus stood quietly, staring out toward the water. Suddenly, I saw a bubbling in the water, effervescent and sparkling.

Curious, I noticed that the net was filling up with fish. "Simon, come here!"

He moved quickly over to me, and we watched more and more fish filling up the net. "Andrew, hurry, grab the end of the net."

There were so many fish in the net now that we were afraid that it would tear. Simon called out to our friends, James and John, in the other boat, "Come and help us."

By the time the other boat came alongside, the nets were so full that they were about to burst. All of us started pulling the nets in, filling both of our boats to the brim with fish almost causing the boats to sink. Right in the midst of all of this, Simon fell to his knees in the middle of all of the fish and said, *"Lord, please leave me— I'm too much of a sinner to be around you"* (Luke 5:8 NLT).

Jesus shook his head and smiled saying, *"Don't be afraid. From now on you'll be fishing for people."* (Luke 5:10 NLT).

And so, it happened. We pulled our boats onto the shore, left everything, and followed Jesus.

Peter's Mother-in-Law

Chapter Five

Capernaum—Home Of Simon And Andrew—John 1:44

After Jesus left the synagogue with James and John, they went to Simon and Andrew's home. 3Now Simon's mother-in-law was sick in bed with a high fever. They told Jesus about her right away. So, he went to her bedside, took her by the hand, and helped her sit up. Then the fever left her, and she prepared a meal for them. That evening after sunset, many sick and demon-possessed people were brought to Jesus. The whole town gathered at the door to watch. So, Jesus healed many people who were sick with various diseases, and he cast out many demons. But because the demons knew who he was, he did not allow them to speak.

Before daybreak the next morning, Jesus got up and went out to an isolated place to pray. Later Simon and the others went out to find him. When they found him, they said, "Everyone is looking for you." But Jesus replied, "We must go on to other towns as well, and I will preach to them, too. That is why I came." So, he traveled throughout the region of Galilee, preaching in the synagogues and casting out demons Mark 1:29-39 (NLT).

*****

T he sun had not yet risen when I woke to the sound of Simon shuffling around the room. There was a loud crash, and I heard Simon swearing.

"Shh, Simon," Miriam whispered. "You will wake the entire household."

"That blasted pot was in my way," Simon whispered back hoarsely.

I lay on my pallet smiling to myself. There was no sleeping once Simon began to stir. His bulk served him well on his fishing boat, but he was truly like a fish out of water on land.

There were more muffled sounds as Simon continued dressing and then quiet after he left the house to complete his morning ritual. Wide-awake now, I rose to light a lamp so that I, too, might begin my day.

Miriam smiled at me sleepily. "Yahweh's blessing on this day, Mother," she said.

"It will be a good one, my daughter."

I gathered the bowl and pestle, filled it with grain, and slipped outside. The sun was coming up, promising to be a beautiful day. A soft wind was blowing off the water bringing with it a bouquet rich with the smells of the sea. I breathed in deeply, never tiring of this sweet fragrance.

Sitting down on the ground, I began to grind the grain, enjoying the repetitive motions of the familiar task. Every morning I spent this time praying to Yahweh and planning my day.

The sea was resplendent this morning; sparkling like diamonds as the sun peeked out between the hills, reflecting its warm rays on the water. There were already fishermen in their boats flinging their nets into the sea, the low murmur of their voices echoing clearly across the water. My eyes closed as I listened to the familiar sounds, my mind wandering as I began to grind the grain. So much has happened in the last few years.

For the most part, life is good for us in Capernaum. Simon and his brother, Andrew, make their living fishing. They moved here as young men from Bethsaida. Simon, of course, is my son-in-law. He and Miriam have been married ten years now, a match that fits both of them well.

I moved in with my daughter and son-in-law two summers ago after my husband was drowned in one of the terrible storms that often take fishermen unaware on the Sea of Galilee. My husband, Seth, enjoyed fishing at night, often going out late with his best friend and partner, Zebedee. Seth and Zebedee grew up together along these shores, small boys learning the ancient trade of their fathers and their grandfathers. They continued to be friends as adults. We danced at each other's weddings and rejoiced at the birth of our children. Zebedee's sons, James and John, were playmates of Miriam.

On the night of the storm, Zebedee came over to tell Seth that he would not be going out with him to fish.

"Wait until tomorrow night, and then I will go with you."

Seth laughed and said, "The fish call me tonight, my friend. I can feel in my bones that this will be a good night."

Zebedee shook his head and laughed saying, "Give those old bones a rest. They work too hard."

Good-naturedly, Seth replied, "Come back tomorrow morning and help me with my large haul, old man."

With that, Zebedee slapped Seth on the back and said, "My wife is keeping my bed warm. I will see you in the morning."

Knowing that Seth was not to be deterred from his mission, I helped him gather his belongings and walked with him to his boat. Three other men were waiting for him on board, anxious to begin. One called out to Seth as we approached. "You're late. The evening is half gone."

"Patience, my friends. Remember, *'The LORD is my portion; therefore, I will wait for him'*" (Lamentations 3:24 NIV).

The Sea of Galilee was especially beautiful that evening. The cerulean sky spread out, draped with glorious shades of pink and gold. The wind had died down and the sea mirrored the dazzling sunset. I watched as Seth helped the men haul huge nets into the boat, his muscles rippling like those of a man half his age. His face was content, always at his happiest on his boat.

Two other boats joined them that evening. They would fish together, banging pans on the side of their boats, herding the schools of fish into a third waiting net.

I held the torches as he lit each one and then placed them at the bow and stern of the small boat. Finally, I handed him a basket filled with bread and dried fish and a flask of wine in case he got hungry or thirsty in the night.

Seth grinned at me and said, "Eliana, come and go with me."

I shook my head. "No, my husband, I am exhausted after this long day. I will have your breakfast waiting for you tomorrow morning."

I watched as they rowed out from shore. The wind would be of no help for him tonight, so he did not unfurl the sail. I sat down on a rock and watched as the small craft slowly made its way out into the deeper water. As it began to grow dark, I squinted to make out the figures in the boats, but all I could see were the torches bobbing up and down in the water. Breathing a prayer for his safety, I reluctantly made my way back home in the dark.

Before retiring that night, I walked outside one more time to look for Seth's boat. The lights were tiny now, as all of the boats had moved further away from the shore. I counted the lights, and satisfied, decided to go to bed.

I woke in the middle of the night to a loud crack of thunder. Worried, I threw on my shawl and went to the door. Peering out, I could see that the wind was coming up and it had started to rain. Soon the rain began coming down in sheets, illuminated now and then by flashes of angry lightning. Praying that Seth had safely moored his boat; I paced the small room waiting for his return. After a time, I could stand it no longer, and throwing a shawl over my head I ventured out into the storm.

I stumbled down the familiar path to the sea; only able to see when the lightning flashed and lit my way. I reached the water and stared at the angry waves; praying, wishing, hoping that Seth's boat would appear.

Fearing the worst, I made my way to Zebedee's home and pounded on the door.

"Zebedee, wake up!" I shouted into the wind.

After a seemingly long time, Zebedee finally came to the door. Seeing me, he quickly opened the door and pulled me inside out of the storm.

"Eliana, what is wrong? Why are you here?"

"Seth has not returned."

Nothing more needed to be said.

"I will wake my sons."

James and John went from house to house to wake the men of the village. They gathered in our house to wait. Storms like this come up suddenly, but do not usually last long. They would be ready.

Seth never did come home. Zebedee and John found his boat shipwrecked along the eastern shore. There was no sign of the crew or my husband—Seth was gone.

Miriam and Simon took me into their home that very day, enveloping me in their love and their busy lives. I grieved deeply for my husband, crying out to Yahweh from the depths of my soul, asking the age-old question—why? At times, the grief was so suffocating that I wished I had gone with Seth that night. Many evenings I would find myself by the sea counting the bobbing lights, wishing that my husband would come home to me. However, as time passed, Yahweh eased my pain, slowly filling the empty void in my heart with the love of my children and grandchildren.

Zebedee and his wife, Salome, continued to be very close to me. Zebedee mourned deeply for his old friend. The three of us talked often, enjoying long walks together along the beach.

*****

With a start, I realized that I was dreaming and not grinding. Simon will never have his breakfast at this pace. As I picked up the pestle and began my task once again, I heard a voice.

"Leave your bowl and come with me. I must talk to you."

It was Zebedee. What would he want from me this early in the morning? He was usually counting the fish that he had caught the night before, getting ready to take his catch to the market.

Hearing the tone in his voice, I laid the stone in the bowl and rose to meet him. Zebedee began to walk briskly toward the beach, and I had to hurry to catch up with him.

"Zebedee, wait!"

Reluctantly, he turned toward me and slowed his pace.

"What is it? What has gotten you so stirred up this morning?"

"Andrew and John. . . . . they're gone. They have left to follow after that prophet . . . . . the man they call "the Baptist."

Stunned, I asked, "Does Simon know? Who will help him on the boat?"

"Who will help me on my boat?" He growled.

"I do not understand. Where did they meet this prophet?"

"He travels along the Jordan River, baptizing and calling people to repentance. John came home several weeks ago from a trip to the south telling us all about this man. He convinced Andrew that he needed to go and meet him."

"Simon is going to be furious with his brother."

"Yes, as I am."

"When did they leave?" I asked.

"Late last night."

Zebedee paused for a moment, staring out toward the water. Finally, he shook his head and frowned saying, "James and the men are waiting for me. I must go."

I nodded. "I will go and tell Simon."

Zebedee left, and I walked slowly back to the house. How am I to break the news to Simon? He will have to hire another man to take his brother's place. Simon is so practical and down to earth. He will not understand why Andrew has left to follow this prophet.

When I returned to the house, Simon was pacing, anxious as usual to get to his nets. I sat down heavily by my bowl and began once again to grind the grain.

"Have you seen Andrew this morning? The day is already half gone, and he has not shown up."

When I did not answer, Simon asked good-naturedly, "What is the matter, old woman? Why so glum on this beautiful day?"

I looked up from my task and said, "Andrew's gone, Simon."

"What do you mean, woman?"

Bracing for Simon's anger, I said quietly, "He left last night with John. Zebedee came by to tell me."

Simon's voice rose. "Where did they go?"

I lay down my pestle and stood up to face him. "They have gone to the Jordan to follow the prophet, John."

Simon's face darkened as he spat out the name. "John! Who is this John?"

"All I know is that he preaches repentance—a turning back to God."

Simon was so angry at this point that I knew it was impossible to explain anything else to him. I sat back down on the ground and began to add water to the meal that I had ground.

"Simon, go gather your nets. I will send Miriam to you with something to eat very soon." I knew that only Miriam had a way of soothing Simon's temper when he was angry like this. Mumbling and cursing under his breath, Simon left for his boat.

✳✳✳✳✳

We did not hear from Andrew for several months. Out of necessity, Simon hired another man to help him on the boat. He spoke little of his brother, spending more time than usual on the sea. Simon and Andrew had always been very close, and we knew that he missed his brother very much.

One evening at dusk, I looked out toward the shore and saw Simon sitting down on a rock with his nets spread out in front of him. Painstakingly, he was working at mending a large hole in one of the nets. His head bowed over his task as his strong hands skillfully weaved the tattered strings of the net. He was so intent that he did not see or hear his brother approach. For a moment, Andrew stood by silently, obviously hesitant to catch Simon's attention. Finally, he walked up to Simon and sat down beside him on the rock. They sat there for some time, talking quietly as they worked together over the net. I do not know what Andrew said to Simon, but they walked arm in arm back to the house smiling and laughing like old times.

It seemed that life would now get back to normal, but that was not to be. Andrew was different somehow, restless. Simon sensed this and often became impatient with him. One evening I asked Andrew to tell us about John. He looked at me and then nervously at Simon. I smiled at him and encouraged him to speak.

"He is a holy man," Andrew spoke timidly at first. "Do you recall what the Prophet Isaiah said?

'Behold, I send My messenger
before Your face,

*Who will prepare Your way
before You'"* (Mark 1:2, NKJ).

Simon nodded, his attention encouraging Andrew to continue.

"He baptizes with water but says that someone who follows him will baptize with the Holy Spirit."

Simon frowned. "Who is this person?"

Andrew looked directly at Simon and said, "I don't know."

Simon stood up and began pacing around the small room. Miriam frowned at him and then asked, "What does he teach?"

"He preaches repentance."

There was silence in the room.

Finally, breaking the silence, I asked, "Andrew, who comes to listen to this man?"

Andrew continued. "He is intent on preaching his message to whoever might listen. He speaks to everyone from the religious leaders to the people from the countryside.

Andrew hesitated one more time and then said hopefully to Simon, "Come with me and hear for yourself."

"That's impossible, Andrew. Someone must stay here and make a living for this family. I can't go off to listen to some crazy prophet!"

Andrew shrugged, knowing that he could not truly explain this man to Simon. Honestly, he did not understand him either. All he knew was he was to follow him, if only for a short time. God required it.

Andrew left with Zebedee's son, John, the next day.

*****

Six months later Miriam and I were washing clothes with the other women of the village. They were laughing and gossiping as women love to do. I usually do not enter into their conversations, preferring to listen as I go about my chore.

I caught the tail end of one conversation between Anna and Mary. Their husbands were fishermen, but both men were very active at the village temple. My ears perked up because I heard them mention the name, John.

"My husband heard him preach. He was even baptized by the prophet," said Mary.

Anna giggled, "I heard that he was a wild-looking man."

Mary slapped the rock with the skirt that she was washing. "Yes, my husband said as such. He told me that this prophet was dressed in a raggedy coat, tied with a wild animal skin. But when my husband came home last week, he was a changed man."

The women were silent after that, the only sound the trickle of the water as they wrung out their laundry and then piled it in baskets to carry away to hang up to dry. Balancing her basket on her head, Anna motioned for Mary to follow and they left us to finish our chore.

Miriam looked over at me as she gathered her wet clothes. Her beautiful face looked thoughtful and a little bit sad. "Why is it, Mother, that Yahweh speaks more to men than to women?"

I could only shake my head.

Not one to brood on such a matter, she brightened and teased, "But your name, Eliana, means *Yahweh has answered me*. Surely, Yahweh has spoken to you, Mother.

Laughing, I said, "Yes, He tells me that we must go home and start dinner.

*****

Simon was waiting for us when we returned. He was grinning at us as we approached, his huge bulk filling the door portal. As he stepped aside to let us through, we could see Andrew behind him, the same warm grin on his face.

"Andrew." Miriam and I exclaimed at the same time, dropping our baskets and spilling the wet clothes onto the floor.

Andrew gathered us both together in one big hug. It was good to see him. We had missed him so much.

"Have you come home to us, Andrew?" Miriam asked hopefully.

Glancing at Simon, he said, "I have come for my big brother. There is a man that I want him to meet.

Surprised, Miriam and I both looked at Simon.

"Are you going to meet the Baptist, Simon?" I asked curiously.

"No, Andrew has told me about another man."

Confused, I asked, "Who is this other man?"

Andrew spoke and said, "I was with John a week ago, and a man came to be baptized by him. This man was different from all the others. When John saw the man coming toward him, he said, *'The Lamb of God who takes away the sin of the world! This is He of whom I said, 'After me comes a Man who is preferred before me'* (John 1:29, 30, NKJ). Later John told me that he saw *'the Spirit descending from heaven like a dove, and He remained upon Him'* (John 1:32). He called him the 'Son of God.'"

Andrew paused and after a moment said, "*We have found the Messiah*" (John 1:41).

No one said anything for a moment. Honestly, I did not know what to think. Miriam placed her arm in Simon's and leaned against him. I sat down heavily on the stool by the door.

Simon broke the silence by saying, "I must go and meet this man."

Miriam moved away and began picking up the clothes that we had spilled on the floor. I continued to sit there and watch dumbly as Miriam juggled her basket of clothes on her hip and moved into the other room.

Finally, with a sigh, I got up and began to prepare the evening meal.

*****

Andrew and Simon were gone the next morning when Miriam and I awoke. We did not speak of it, pretending that it was a morning like any other. I kept going to the door to look out toward the sea, drawn to the sight of Simon's boat rocking gently in the waves. It looked lonely somehow with its wilted nets draped over the side of the boat like an old woman's headscarf. I could hear the other fishermen's voices echoing to each other across the lake. Why would Simon leave his boat to go with Andrew? I asked myself repeatedly. Simon never even left his boat when he was sick, choosing to fish even on the coldest and most miserable of days. What possessed him to leave now? I could not even imagine it. Throughout that long day, Miriam's face mirrored my thoughts. We were both scared and uneasy. Somehow, we knew that our life was about to change.

"And The Report About Him Went Out Into Every Place

In The Surrounding Region" (Luke 4:37).

The next morning Miriam went into Capernaum to purchase oil for our lamps. She was gone until mid-morning, returning with news of the Rabbi, Jesus of Nazareth.

"People are talking of this Rabbi," she said.

"What do you hear?" I asked curiously.

"They are saying that he was physically thrown out of the town of Nazareth two Sabbaths ago."

"For what reason?"

"He speaks with authority and no one likes it."

"With what authority?" I was not going to let this go.

"He says, '*Repent, for the Kingdom of God is at hand.*'"

I shook my head and said nothing.

"I am worried about Simon, Mother. Do you think he and Andrew are now with this man?"

★★★★★

Simon and Andrew were gone for a long month, finally coming home one Sabbath eve. I was especially tired that evening and was lying down on my pallet at the back of the house. Concerned, Miriam had come to see about me.

"Are you not feeling well, Mother?" she asked. Miriam knelt down and gently touched my cheek with the back of her hand. Her hand felt cool on my face.

Frowning, she said, "I think you have a fever."

Before I could speak, we heard a loud and familiar voice. "Miriam, where are you? We are home."

I struggled to my feet as Miriam ran into the other room.

When I finally reached the front of the house,

Miriam was still engulfed in Simon's embrace. Andrew grinned when he saw me appear and then quickly had a look of concern on his face.

"You don't look well, Eliana," he said.

"Mother," Miriam said sternly. "You must go back to bed."

Frowning like a spoiled child, I said, "Let me just sit here and visit for a while. I am sure that I will be all right. I want to hear about this man that took you away from us, Simon."

Simon and Andrew exchanged glances, their faces alight with pleasure and excitement. I have honestly never seen either of them look so energized.

"We want you both to meet him," Simon said.

"What is his name?" Miriam asked.

"His name is Jesus of Nazareth."

"Tell us about him, Simon. What draws you to this man?" I asked.

Miriam nodded her head looking from Simon to Andrew. "Yes, I want to know, also."

There was a long silence. Simon walked to the door and stared out toward the sea. Finally, he spoke. "After Andrew and I left last month, I kept asking myself why I was so interested in meeting this man. I am a fisherman, not a holy man. I belong on a boat, not following some prophet. I almost talked myself into turning around and coming home several times."

"Where did you find him?" Miriam cut in.

"We had heard that he was close to Bethabara. Everywhere we traveled, the people were talking about John the Baptist and a man named Jesus of Nazareth. We came upon him one evening along the banks of the Jordan. Andrew and I were tired from our travels and decided to stop for the night at a ford that is a popular camping place for travelers. Andrew noticed a group of John's disciples settling down for the night, so we decided to join them."

Andrew nodded and said, "It was getting dark, but I spotted him immediately. He was sitting off to himself watching as the travelers arrived and settled into the camp. I caught Simon's attention and nodded in Jesus' direction. At that moment, he stood and walked over to us."

Simon shook his head, looking down at the ground as if still not believing what had happened. Finally, he looked up and took Miriam's hand beside him. "Miriam, how can I explain this all to you?

Miriam sat quietly and waited for Simon to continue.

"We stood as he approached. He was an ordinary-looking man—a typical Galilean with short brown hair, squarely built and strong in the shoulders. He walked up to us as if we were old friends stretching out his hand and grasping Andrew's hand and then mine. When he shook my hand and looked into my eyes, he said, "You are Simon, the son of John—but you will be called Cephas."

Miriam frowned and said, "Cephas? Peter? The Rock? Why did he call you that?"

"I'm not sure," Simon admitted honestly. "All I know is my boat and fishing—and life in Galilee. I know you—Eliana—and I know Andrew. What do I know of the future? Now I have met someone who may not only change my life but all of yours, too. I feel like I am being pulled toward something that I have no control over."

Miriam looked perplexed. She slowly shook her head and looked at Simon. "I don't know what you're saying. I don't understand any of this."

Gently, Simon put his arm around Miriam and pulled her close to his side.

Andrew continued the conversation. "We sat around a small fire talking until late into the night. Jesus' voice and words captivated us because he had so much wisdom and knowledge about God. He told us that after John baptized him, the Spirit of God led him into the Wilderness where he ate nothing at all for forty days and nights. At the end of that time, the Devil, himself, appeared to him." Andrew's voice trailed off. He glanced at Simon and then toward me, his face reflecting concern that he had said too much.

Despite my fever, I felt a cold shiver go through me. I wrapped my shawl closer around me and laid my head back against the wall. Eying Andrew, I asked skeptically, "Who is this man that the Devil would appear to him?"

Andrew hesitated and then continued. "The Devil tempted Jesus to use his power in a way that was contrary to God's will for him."

Sensing my doubt, Simon interrupted by changing the subject. "Enough about all of that, there is so much more to tell you. We left the following morning with Jesus, traveling with him to a wedding in Cana. On the way, more men joined us."

"Yes, Philip was first," Andrew explained. "He joined us in Galilee. He was from our hometown of Bethsaida."

Nathanael Of Cana From Galilee – John 21:10

Simon smiled and said, "The next day, Philip met a man by the name of Nathanael. The four of us had stopped for a noonday meal close to the town of Cana.

We were hot, thirsty, and looking for some shade to get out of the sun for a while. We spotted a cluster of fig trees along the side of the road; thinking that their low branches looked inviting, a respite to us from the noon-day sun. We stretched out beneath one of the trees to rest and shared our meal of figs and bread. Jesus, Andrew, and I soon dozed off, drowsy after our good meal while Philip wandered off to speak to others hunkered down under the other fig trees."

Andrew continued. "After a short while, I heard Jesus stir, so I opened one eye to see what was going on. He was sitting up and staring toward another tree. I said something to him, but he did not answer me. Curious, I sat up and followed his gaze to see Philip talking ani-matedly with a man who kept looking our way. Philip was gesturing toward us and seemed to be inviting the man to join us. He looked toward us, shook his head, and then said something to Philip."

Simon laughed and interrupted, "It seems that he had asked Philip if anything good could come out of Naz-areth."

Smiling, Andrew continued his dialogue. "Phillip told him to 'Come and See'. When they walked over to us, Jesus said, '*Behold, an Israelite indeed, in whom is no deceit!*'"

I interrupted at that point. "How did he know this about Nathanael?"

"Nathanael was surprised, also," Andrew said. "He asked Jesus '*how do you know me?*'"

"Jesus told him, '*Before Philip called you, I saw you under the fig tree.*'"

Simon joined in the conversation again. "Natha-nael addressed Jesus as the Son of God and King of Israel."

There was a silence in the room after Simon spoke.

I felt an icy fear creep into my old bones as I contemplated what Simon had just said.

Simon stood up and began to pace the room as he is apt to do when agitated or has something on his mind.

"Jesus laughed at the fact that Nathanael was impressed that he saw him under the fig tree. He said to Nathanael, '*You will see greater things than these. You will see heaven open, and the angels of God ascending and descending upon the Son of Man.*'"

Miriam spoke up finally. It is truly not like her to be so quiet. There was fear in her voice when she said, "Simon, men have died for saying less than this. Who is this man?"

I could not sit there any longer. My head was pounding, and all I could think about was my nice soft pallet and laying my head down on my pillow. Slowly I rose to my feet and padded off to the other room. The others went to bed shortly thereafter.

I felt much better the next morning. Simon and Andrew got up early to check on their boat and began the process of gathering their nets to fish the following evening. Miriam sang to herself as she prepared the morning meal.

"Good morning, Mother," she said happily. "Are you feeling well?"

I smiled at her and nodded. "I'm feeling much better today. For some reason, this fever seems to come and go. I never really know when I will be feeling bad. It has seemed to come more often lately, though."

Miriam looked at me closely and frowned. "I worry about you, Mother."

I patted her on the back and walked outside to retrieve a pot that I had left by the door last night.

Several weeks passed by. It was comforting to fall back into a routine. Simon and Andrew seemed content to be back on their boat, and of course, Miriam was delighted to have Simon home. Soon, however, my health began to decline even more. The fever was now constantly plaguing me, and each day I spent more and more time on my pallet. One morning, I could not even lift my head. Miriam and Simon did not know what to do to help me. There were times when I did not even recognize Miriam as she faithfully tried to spoon a little soup into my mouth. At other times, I was all too aware of my pounding head and aching body.

One evening as I was resting, Simon knelt beside my bed and took my hand. "Eliana," he whispered gently. "I saw Jesus today."

I opened my eyes to see Simon kneeling beside me with tears rolling down his face. I squeezed his rough, calloused hand and whispered hoarsely, "Tell me about him, Simon."

"Andrew and I had come in from a night of fishing. We were washing the nets and stretching them out to dry. James and John were there, also, laughing and joking, as they love to do. We did not have much luck fishing, so we were discussing where we could fish the next night that might prove more profitable. We heard a commotion behind us and turned to see a large crowd of people following a man who was coming our way. As he strode closer to us, I realized that the man was Jesus."

Simon laid my hand down and then made himself more comfortable, at least as comfortable as a man his size could be sitting on the floor.

Luke 5

"He walked over to us and asked me if we could put

out a little from the land. So, the three of us waded out to the boat and climbed in."

Simon laughed and then said, "Eliana, you know that James and John will not be left behind, so they pushed their boat out alongside ours."

I could only smile and nod my head. James and John always wanted to be in the middle of everything.

"When we were a short distance from the shore, Andrew threw out the anchor, and we sat down to listen. The crowd was so still that they almost blended in with the shore. There was barely a breeze to even ripple the water or rock the boat. Jesus also sat down and taught the multitudes from the boat. His words rang out clear and true, but it was his message that echoed in my heart."

"When He had stopped speaking, He said to me, *'Launch out into the deep and let down your nets for a catch.'*"

"I said to him, *'Master, we have toiled all night and caught nothing; nevertheless, at Your word, I will let down the net.'*"

"I caught Andrew's eye as he raised an eyebrow at me. He grinned and shrugged as he helped me lift our anchor, and we rowed out toward the deeper part of the lake. We were both quiet as we rowed, concentrating on our destination and Jesus as he stood at the bow looking out toward the water."

"We did not go far before Jesus pointed to a place where we had fished the night before. Still skeptical, I nodded to Andrew and he began to pull out the nets from the bottom of the boat."

"Jesus told us again to let down our nets. When we did, immediately the nets began to fill up with fish. It was incredible. Andrew and I both looked at each other in astonishment as Jesus laughed and began helping us pull in the nets. Soon, I realized that our boat could not even begin to hold all of those fish. James and John were not too far away, so we hollered at them, 'Come and help us!' All we could do was to hold on until they got there."

Simon shook his head, his face wreathed in a huge smile. "Eliana, it was unbelievable. After James and John arrived with their boat, we filled both boats so full of fish that I feared we would sink. We all stood there for a moment and stared at those fish. Even James and John were speechless. Overcome with the miracle of it all, I fell to my knees in the middle of that huge mass of fish and cried, '*Depart from me, for I am a sinful man, O Lord!*' Jesus reached down, helped me to my feet, and said, '*Do not be afraid. From now on you will catch men.*'"

Simon paused and stared out the door, lost in his thoughts. Finally, he shook his head and said, "I still do not believe what happened."

I looked up at Simon, amazed at the change in my son-in-law. This gruff, no-nonsense fisherman had been transformed into someone I did not even know. "Simon, what does this mean?"

"I must follow Jesus, Eliana."

I squeezed his hand and closed my eyes as sleep overcame me once more.

Luke 4:38-39

The next few days were lost to me as the fever took its toll on my body. The first I remember was a voice calling to me from far away. I had never heard that voice before, but then again it sounded very familiar.

"Eliana." The sound of it was like a cool breeze blowing over me.

"Eliana!" Now the voice was hovering over me, the power of it vibrating into my very being.

Confused and trying desperately to focus my eyes, I asked, "Simon? Miriam? Is that you?"

Someone picked up my right hand and enclosed it snugly in theirs.

It is difficult to describe the sensation that came into my body at that moment. At once, I felt an incredible wellness—strength poured into my limbs. I opened my eyes to see the kindest and most caring eyes smiling back at me.

I knew immediately that the man holding my hand and smiling at me was Jesus. I smiled back at him as he helped me gently to my feet.

I stood up gingerly, thinking that I must be very weak after lying in the bed for so many days. Jesus let go of my hand, and Miriam stepped up quickly to hold my arm. Instead of feeling feeble or dizzy, my legs felt strong, and I was completely clear-headed.

"Mother?" Miriam looked at me with concern.

Amazed, I reached out and hugged Jesus and then Miriam. Laughing and praising God, I said, "Miriam, it is time for our noonday meal. We must serve our friends."

The Wedding at Cana

Chapter Six

John 2:1-12

I t is my wedding day. Like every young Jewish girl, I have dreamed often of this day. My family is so pleased with our match, and perhaps I will even fall in love. Of course, I will. God has blessed me with a wonderful man. His name is James. My name is Rachel. I have always felt good about my name and believed that God would give me a good and kind man, one like our forefather Jacob who waited seven years to marry his Rachel. James and I have been betrothed now for six months. He has spent these last few months building a house for us to live in. He treats me with respect, and dare I hope, love?

So much preparation; everything must be perfect. My Aunt Mary is coming to help. I have heard that she may bring her son, Jesus. We have invited both Jesus and his disciples. I hope Jesus' brothers and sisters come also. It has been a long time since we have all been together.

I'm sure Jesus still thinks of me as that little girl who followed him around, toting hammers and nails, *helping.* He was always very patient with me. One day I was trying, unsuccessfully, to hammer together a box. My brother informed me that girls were not carpenters and ridiculed my efforts. Finding me in tears, Jesus knelt beside me, eye to eye. Ashamed, I tried to hide my tears from him. He told me that God knew and cared about me, even when I was disappointed or angry. I looked at him in surprise and told him frankly that God had more important things to worry about than me. Besides, I was a girl, and surely God did not think much of girls. Jesus threw his head back and laughed. "Rachel," he said kindly, "God created you to be a girl, even giving you a name before you were born."

I looked at him incredulously, narrowing my eyes and thinking that he was making fun of me, but there was a genuine look of concern and love in his eyes.

"Come, let me show you how to make that birdhouse."

Walking hand in hand with him, I wondered how he knew my little clumsy box was supposed to be a birdhouse?

But that was eight years ago. There is still much preparation to be done for my wedding. I must stop this daydreaming and get busy. My father is borrowing and gathering together the huge pots used for ceremonial washing. There must be plenty of them, for the entire village will be invited to the celebration. We must calculate the right amount of food and drink for the guests. In the meantime, my mother is busy sewing the last few coins on my beautiful headdress.

The wedding ceremony will take place this evening, and then there will be dancing, feasting, and drinking for an entire week. It will be so much fun, and I will feel like a queen.

"Rachel, Rachel." My little sister, Anna, burst into the house, her eyes shining with pleasure and excitement. "Aunt Mary and Jesus are here. And Jesus has brought five friends. I have already learned their names. They are Andrew, John, Philip, Nathaniel, and Simon."

Anna was talking so fast that I could hardly understand her. With the bluntness of a child, she blurted out, "Will we have enough food and wine for them, Rachel?"

"Hush, Anna," I frowned. "We must not embarrass our guests. Come and take me to them, so that I might greet them, also."

I walked out into the courtyard to see Jesus standing and talking to Aunt Mary and his five friends. They were all laughing, relaxed, and at ease with each other. I did not know the men, but it seemed like they must have been friends with Jesus for a very long time.

Mary embraced me with a smile and a kiss. "Rachel, may God bless you on your wedding day." Then with the take-charge attitude of a Jewish mother, she said, "I am here to help you. Where is that brother of mine? I must find out what to do and get busy doing it."

I smiled and said, "Father is filling the ceremonial pots, Aunt Mary. He will be so glad to know that you are here. There is still so much to do."

I then turned toward Jesus and embraced him. "Jesus, thank you for coming to my wedding."

He grinned at me and then introduced his friends. "This is my little cousin, Rachel. She is a master birdhouse builder."

I blushed and explained to the men, "Jesus is a wonderful teacher."

Standing quietly by all of this time, Anna could stand it no longer. "Jesus, I am to show you and your friends where you will be staying. Aunt Mary, you will be staying here with us."

The men followed Anna while Aunt Mary and I went to find Father.

The afternoon went by quickly. Soon it was time to dress for the ceremony. My mother and Aunt Mary were there to help me dress. As they placed the beautiful veil over my face, I knew I would never be the same. My carefree, childhood days were now over. I had become a woman.

We were officially married when the wedding veil was taken from my face and placed on James' shoulder. Shyly, I smiled at my bridegroom. He took my hand, and we began the procession through the streets of Cana. People were lining the streets, holding burning torches and lanterns of oil, laughing and shouting best wishes to us. We made our way to James' house and the party began.

What a joyous occasion! I will never forget that week. People came and went all week long, celebrating with us. I saw Jesus and his friends several times. They were all having a wonderful time, dancing and celebrating with the villagers.

The servants kept bringing out more food and wine. On the third day, I heard the servants whispering to each other. I knew something was amiss, so I asked one of them what the problem might be.

"We are running out of wine," he explained.

How could this be? I knew that there had been careful consideration as they prepared for the expected crowd.

It would be humiliating to my family and James if we ran out of wine. Aunt Mary walked up as I was talking to the servants. I explained the situation to her. She patted my shoulder and smiled. "I will take care of this,

Rachel."

Mary found Jesus at the party. It was never hard to spot him because he was always in the middle of a crowd of people. She walked up to Jesus and waited politely as he finished telling a story. At the end of the story, he threw back his head and laughed with the easy laugh of someone who was enjoying himself. She smiled and said, "My son, may I speak to you?"

Taking him aside, Mary explained that there was no more wine.

Jesus looked intently at his mother and said respectfully, *"Woman, why do you ask me to do this? My time has not yet come"* (John 2:4 NLT).

They looked at each other for a long moment until Mary finally reached out and squeezed Jesus on the arm. He nodded at her.

She turned to the servants nearby and said, "Do what he tells you to do."

They were all standing by the six ceremonial pots that had been used all week for cleansing. Jesus told the servants, *"Fill the pots to the brim with water."* The head servant nodded to the others, and they did so. Then Jesus said, *"Now draw some out and take it to the master of the banquet."* The man looked at Jesus, not sure why he was to do such a thing. Jesus smiled at him and then nodded toward the pots. "Go ahead," he said quietly. Shrugging his shoulders, the servant dipped the dipper into the pot. At first, he could not believe what he saw, so he dipped into the pot again. Gesturing for another servant to bring a pitcher, he poured a rich ruby-red liquid into it. The servants were stunned, looking at Jesus with awe and maybe a little fear.

They took the pitcher of liquid and set it down in

front of the master of the banquet. I was sitting there beside James, not really paying attention to what was happening. Then I heard the master say in a surprised voice, "This is an excellent wine. Most people serve the best wine first, and then after everyone has had their fill, they bring in the cheap wine." He held up his cup to us and said, "To the bride and groom!"

The servants stood by, smiling knowingly at each other. We did not even realize what had happened until the next day when word spread throughout the village that Jesus had turned water into wine.

I did not see him again that week. It was said that he left soon after he had turned the water into wine.

Who was this cousin of mine? There had been whispers throughout the years concerning the circumstances of his birth. But those had died down long before he settled into his job as a carpenter in Nazareth. I heard many stories about him after my wedding. People were saying that he might even be the Messiah. We heard that he came back through Cana several months after my wedding and healed the son of an official of the king's court.

Jesus visited our home soon after that. We were so glad that he came by because we had many questions to ask him. James and I talked with him until late into the night. He left the next morning. James and I knew in our hearts that this man had changed our lives as surely as he had changed the water into wine. We would never be the same.

The Healing of the Paralytic

Chapter Seven

Matthew 9:1-8; Mark 2:1-12; Luke 5:17-26

"He's back." Thomas ran breathlessly up to me on the street.

"Who is?" I asked.

"The man, Jesus of Nazareth. He is at Peter's house."

I looked at him, and we both nodded. It was time. Our friend, Joshua, could wait no longer. He was desperately in need of healing. But would he let us help him? Would he allow himself to hope? He had been so depressed after the accident that paralyzed him and caused his brother, Isaac, to lose his life. They had both been foolish, but Joshua had blamed himself for his brother's death. Each day he sunk deeper into his pallet. We were going to lose him, too, if something didn't happen soon. We would make it happen.

Calling two more of our friends, Seth and James, we went into the house to carry Joshua to Jesus. The look in his eyes as we approached was not encouraging.

"We're taking you to the Rabbi Jesus. We think he can heal you," I explained.

"Leave me alone. It will be of no use," our friend replied.

We had been friends for years, growing up together as children along the Sea of Galilee, six boisterous, young men living life to its fullest. Now there were only five of us. We could not let it become four.

Grabbing hold of each corner of the pallet, we lifted Joshua and went out the door. It was only a short distance to Peter's house. The house was located along the beach on the Sea of Galilee. Our enthusiasm was tempered as we walked up to the house with our load. People were everywhere. They were milling around outside, climbing onto the roof, and into the windows. There were several hundred people between Jesus and us. What were we going to do now? There was no way anyone would let us in the door carrying Joshua on the pallet. Even if we waited, there would probably be too much confusion when Jesus left the house, and who knew when that would be?

Seth joked, "Let's tear off the roof and go in that way." Andrew, James, Seth, and I looked at each other. "Why not?" With all the confidence of youth, we hoisted Joshua up onto the roof. Laying the pallet gently down, we began chipping at the roof. Chunks of clay and thatch began flying. We pulled at the branches, unmindful of the mess we were making. By that time others on the roof joined in to help us.

When we finally broke through the ceiling, I stuck my head in the hole and looked inside. We were right above Jesus. He looked up amidst the pieces of plaster, clay, and dust. Squinting up at me, he smiled. I thought he would be furious at the intrusion, but his smile encouraged me. I turned back to my friends. "It's okay," I said. We began to pull away larger chunks of the roof, enough to lift Joshua and his pallet through the opening.

For the first time, Joshua looked hopeful, his face easing from the pain that came more from the spirit than from the body. Several including Jesus grabbed at the mat as we began to lower him through the roof. After lowering Joshua to the floor, Jesus knelt beside him and glanced up at Seth, James, Andrew, and me and smiled at us, as if saying, "It's all right, just calm down, I see your faith." He then looked down at Joshua and said, *"Son, your sins are forgiven"* (Luke 5:20 NLT).

I looked at my friend on the pallet, his eyes locked on Jesus, and I could see his body finally relax. There was relief in the expression on his face. Jesus stayed close to his side, his hand remaining on his shoulder. Something began happening that only Jesus, Joshua, and I noticed. It was as if all the anger, depression, and hurt that Joshua felt over his brother's death began to lift from his body. He was forgiven. It was really "all right". He was forgiven for his foolishness and the impetuousness that he felt had caused the accident.

Jesus glanced down one more time and then up at the crowd. *"But that you may know that the Son of Man has power on earth to forgive sins . . ."* He looked at Joshua and continued, *"I say to you, arise, take up your bed, and go to your house"* (Luke 5:24). Joshua looked at me, and I believed with him. There was a gasp from the crowd as Joshua stood up, picked up his pallet, and began walking through the crowded room and out the door. We were in total shock at what had just happened. I stood there and stared. Finally, Seth hit me on the shoulder, breaking my trance. He shouted, "Come on, let's go. Praise God!" Joshua was healed. We turned around before we left and looked one more time at Jesus. He was laughing and gestured for us to join our friend.

On the way out, we passed Peter at the door. "Peter, we'll be back to fix your roof, we promise. Right now, we're going to help Joshua start living again." From the look on Peter's face, I knew he understood.

The Calling of Levi

Chapter Eight

Matthew 9:9-13; Mark 2:13-17; Luke 5:27-32

My name is Levi. My job is to collect taxes for the Romans. It is not a job that has made me very popular, but it is one that has made me very rich. For a while, I enjoyed my prosperity, really the only thing I had left after my family and friends turned their backs on me. I made new friends; tax collectors like me.

One morning, I was at my booth, going about my business, ignoring the usual complaints of the people, when I heard a commotion in the street. People were laughing, talking, and cheering about the healing of a young man who had been paralyzed in an accident. They said he was now walking again. What is this nonsense? I knew that young man. I had even talked to his parents after the tragic accident that took his brother's life and left him paralyzed.

I listened from my booth as I heard the people talk about how Jesus had not only healed the boy but also had forgiven his sins. Sins, I mused. What does a young man know of sin? How could he know how it could pull a person down and take control of his life? I closed my ears and heart to all that I heard.

Dismissing all of this, I turned back to my books. I was so engrossed in my numbers, that I did not realize someone was standing in front of me until I heard him call my name. "Good afternoon, Levi." I immediately began to speculate as to who this person was, if I had seen him before, and most importantly if I was to collect taxes from him.

He spoke to me, *"Follow me"* (Matthew 9:9). Nothing more was said or needed to be said. What was happening to me? I got up from behind my booth, left my ledgers and my bills, and followed him. We went to my house where it was quiet, and we began to talk. He shared many things with me—with me, "Levi, the hated", "Levi, the tax collector". Why did he care about me? Why would he want me to be a follower? So many questions I had. This made no sense to me.

We talked until late in the afternoon. I knew that I wanted my friends to hear what he had to say. I decided to hold a great banquet and invite them to meet Jesus. Would they come? Of course, if there were food and drink. Would they listen to him? I didn't know.

I sent servants out to invite my friends to come to the banquet the following evening. I hoped they would come out of curiosity, if for no other reason. These people were not the most popular in society. They were sinners in the eyes of the Pharisees. Of course, I was one too.

They arrived the next evening, curious about meeting the man, Jesus. Many had already heard about him. Soon after everyone had arrived, a group of Pharisees walked into my courtyard. They couldn't believe that Jesus was here at my house. "Look at him," one of the Pharisees said. "He eats with sinners, tax collectors, publicans—the dregs of society."

Jesus went over to the man, looked him straight in the eye, and said softly, *"It is not the healthy who need a doctor, but the sick. For I did not come to call the righteous, but sinners, to repentance"* (Matthew 9:13).

And so, I have been called. I, Matthew, yes, the very same Levi, left everything to follow my Lord. I was there through it all. I was chosen to record the events of my Lord Jesus Christ. God used my intellect and my gifts to record His life. How grateful I am that he chose me. The God of the Universe chose me.

Andrew and the Boy with the Loaves and Fishes

Chapter Nine

Matthew 14:13-21; Mark 6:30-44; Luke 9:10-17; John 6:1-15

"Sir, where are you going? May I go, too?"

Eagerly, the small, raggedy little boy followed me as I left the marketplace. His mother was selling bread and fish from a tiny booth at the end of the street.

His name was Simon, and we had become friends several days earlier when Jesus, the other disciples, and I arrived in Capernaum.

Simon was no more than nine years old, small and wiry, his eyes dancing with untold mischief and intelligence. He started following me around when he heard that I was with the miracle worker, Jesus. He loved running errands for us and was constantly asking questions. Sometimes Simon was a help to us, but more often than not, he was a nuisance.

The other disciples were not quite as patient as I, mainly ignoring the child as adults were prone to do. As I said earlier, Simon loved to ask questions. He had heard about some of the miracles of Jesus and would badger me with one question after another.

One day I asked, "Simon, would you like to meet the Master?" His eyes lit up and a huge grin spread across his face. That was answer enough for me. He grabbed my hand and pulled me half running through the market-place to the beach where Jesus was sitting and talking with the disciples.

Jesus smiled as we walked up. "Andrew, bring your young friend over here to join us." Simon sat down beside me trying very hard not to wiggle, but not doing a very good job of it. Finally, bored with our adult conversation, he picked up some pebbles and began tossing them into the water.

Distracted, one of the disciples frowned at Simon and then asked Jesus, *"Who is the greatest in the kingdom of heaven"* (Matthew 18:1 NIV)?

Jesus paused for a moment and then called out, "Simon, come over here for a minute."

Surprised and delighted that he had been noticed, Simon dropped his pebbles and skipped over to Jesus. Jesus put his arm around his shoulders and said, *"I tell you the truth, unless you change and become like little children, you will never enter the kingdom of heaven. Therefore, whoever humbles himself like this child is the greatest in the kingdom of heaven."*

He looked at Simon and then back at the disciples and continued, *"And whoever welcomes a little child like this in my name welcomes me"* (Matthew 18:3-5 NIV).

That was two days ago. Today we are crossing to the other side of the Sea of Galilee. Simon wanted to tag along with us. I told him to run to the market and ask his mother if she would pack him some food because we would not be back for several days. He hurried away and returned with a sack bursting with bread and fish.

"This will hold us for a few days, Andrew."

I smiled at him. "Come, Simon, let's go find the Master."

We followed Jesus to the mountain slope that rose above the Sea of Galilee. Jesus stood at the top of the slope looking down toward us and out toward the sea. People began gathering all along the mountain, bringing the lame, the blind, the crippled, and many others. Simon moved importantly through the crowd, helping to lead the people to the Master.

One day turned into another until three days had already gone by. The crowd had grown to almost five thousand men, not counting their wives and children, scattered along the grassy slope.

Late on the afternoon of the third day, Jesus looked across the crowd and said to Philip, who was from the area, "These people are hungry. Where shall we buy bread for them to eat?"

Philip looked at the crowd and shook his head. *"Eight months' wages would not buy enough bread for each one to have a bite!"* (John 6:7 NIV).

Simon was sitting by me during this conversation. He started yanking on my robe. With a grin on his face, Simon held up what was left of his bread and fish. Jokingly, I entered the conversation by saying, "Simon has five small barley loaves and two small fish left."

Resolutely, Jesus said, *"Make the people sit down"* (John 6:10).

Five thousand men plus their wives and children sat down on the beautiful slope, their backs to the Sea of Galilee, their faces toward Jesus.

Jesus asked Simon if he would share his food with the crowd. Eagerly, Simon jumped up and ran over to

Jesus and placed the sack of fish and bread in his hand.

"Thank you, Simon; may God bless your generosity. Now would you help us distribute the food?"

With a face-splitting grin, Simon nodded vigorously. Standing proudly beside Jesus, he waited patiently as Jesus took the loaves and gave thanks. He then helped us distribute the food. As we did, we noticed that there was more food now than before Jesus prayed. The more we gave out, the more we had to give.

The people were laughing and talking, enjoying the picnic. As one group finished eating, we gathered up their leftovers and served another group. The more people ate, the more leftovers we had to feed other families.

Several hours later, Simon ran up to me, his sack still bursting with bread and fish. "Andrew, are you hungry?" He was grinning from ear to ear. Finally, we sat down together and ate our fill.

"You have done well, my little friend. The disciples and I must leave now. I have arranged for you to go home with a family from your town. Jesus has asked us to get into the boat and leave before the crowd begins to stir."

"But, Andrew, I am a disciple, too! Can't I go with you?"

Smiling at him, I knelt down eye to eye and said, "Yes, Simon, you are truly a disciple now. But you must go back home and tell others about what you have seen here today. There will come a day when the Master will need your help once again. Now, your mother needs you to take care of her. We will meet again, my friend; I am sure of it."

With that lopsided grin, Simon grabbed his sack, still full, and ran to join the others.

Leah

Chapter Ten

Mark 5:21-43; Luke 8:40-56; Matthew 9:18-26

"Leah, where are you?"

I was sitting in the courtyard, dozing in the warm, late afternoon sun.

"Leah, are you there? Leah!"

My sister continued to call my name until roused from my nap, I answered sleepily, "Yes, Rebecca, I am in the courtyard."

Rebecca rushed into the courtyard. Her face, which was usually wreathed in a huge smile, was somber. My sister was the light of my life and my contact with the outside world. I did not leave my house very often because of an illness that I had endured for twelve years. I could always count on Rebecca to have some kind of news for me.

Shaking the cobwebs from my head, I said, "What is your news this time, Rebecca?" My sister loved to gossip with her friends as they washed clothes or shopped at the market.

"It is said that Jairus' daughter is very, very ill," she explained sadly. "Remember, I have told you about her. She is such a sweet child, totally unaware that she has such a prominent father. I had heard that they are sending for the best doctors."

I shook my head, thinking of doctors. I have certainly seen my share of doctors in the last twelve years. Unfortunately, I did not have much faith in their healing abilities. Their cures had done me no good. On their advice, I had taken tonics and applied astringents. Grimacing at the memory, I remembered even going so far as to carry around the ashes of an ostrich egg in a cotton rag in the winter and a linen rag in the summer. I was embarrassed to think about the time I carried around the barleycorn that Rebecca had found in the dung of a white she-ass. She had convinced me that trying that remedy would definitely cure me.

For twelve years now, I had not been able to worship Yahweh in the synagogue or have any kind of fellowship with my friends. My condition made me as unclean as a leper.

Rebecca looked at me lovingly, gently placing her hand on my shoulder. "How are you feeling today?"

I smiled and patted her hand. "The same, Rebecca, no better and no worse." I motioned for her to sit down. "Come, sit down and tell me more."

Rebecca sat down beside me and began to tell me more about the child's grave condition. She concluded by saying, "I have even heard people say that Jairus needs to send for Jesus."

Surprised at this, I said, "Jesus, the prophet that you told me about?"

Rebecca nodded her head vigorously. "Yes, we have heard that he does all kinds of miracles."

I nodded, remembering the stories that Rebecca told me about him.

"But he is not very popular with Jairus' friends at the synagogue."

"Rebecca," I said eagerly, "tell me again what you have heard of this man, Jesus."

Smiling, she jumped up and began pacing around the room. Her hands, always animated, began flying as she told me about Jesus casting an unclean spirit out of a man in the synagogue.

She paused for a moment and then continued again. "Do you remember me telling you about Jesus healing Simon Peter's mother? What a dear, sweet lady she is."

She walked over and looked out the door into the street. Turning suddenly, she said, "Oh! Leah, I forgot . . . I forgot to tell you the latest that I have heard about Jesus. How could I have forgotten to tell you this?"

"Come and sit down. I patted the seat beside me. You are wearing me out with your pacing. What have you forgotten to tell me?"

She plopped down eagerly at my feet and looked up at me with an infectious grin. I encouraged her to continue.

She began telling me an incredible story about a man called Legion who lived on the other side of the Sea of Galilee in the country of the Gadarenes. He was tormented by many demons. People were afraid of him, so he was bound with shackles and chains. (Luke 8: 26-39).

"Jesus was in a boat with all of his disciples. They were going over to the other side to teach. Legion met Jesus when he got off the boat," she said excitedly.

"What did Jesus do?" I asked curiously.

"You won't believe this, Leah, but Jesus commanded all of those demons to jump into a herd of swine!"

I had to laugh at the thought. "Oh, my. What happened then?"

With her hands gesturing wildly again, Rebecca said, "All of those swine started stampeding and ran off a cliff into the sea."

"The swine herders must have been very angry at that," I said.

"Leah, they were so terrified that they just ran away. But I'm sure when they realized that they had lost all of their livelihood, they must have been furious with Jesus."

"What happened to Legion?"

"When the swine herders came back to the place where it had happened, they saw Legion sitting with Jesus. He was now fully dressed and in his right mind."

I shook my head. "This just does not seem possible."

Rebecca sat down dejected. "I know, Leah, I know."

We sat quietly for a moment, each of us lost in our thoughts.

Breaking the silence, Rebecca jumped up again and said, "I must go now. Simeon is going to be looking all over for me. The last time I came home late, he threatened to add another wife to our family."

I laughed. "Come back soon, Rebecca. You know you always make me laugh and brighten my day."

"I will come and see you again, Sister. Is there anything I can bring you from the market?"

I gave her my list, and she left hurrying out the door. I shook my head. My sister makes me feel very, very old.

I continued to sit quietly after Rebecca left. My

thoughts kept returning to the man, Jesus. Who was he? Were these stories true? Could he possibly be the One that we had been waiting for? Shaking my head, I left the courtyard to light the lamps in preparation for another long and lonely night.

The next day, Rebecca came by the house earlier than usual. "What brings you out so early, Sister?" I asked.

"I am going to the Sea of Galilee. I have heard that Jesus is here in Capernaum. A crowd has gathered down at the beach."

She took me by both hands, "Come and go with me, Leah," she said excitedly.

"You know I can't be out among the crowds, Rebecca. It is forbidden."

"Oh, Leah, just cover your head. No one will even know it is you."

"No, you go on, Rebecca. Come back soon and tell me all about what you see and hear."

Reluctantly, Rebecca let go of my hands, gave me a quick hug, and left.

The house was so quiet. I wandered from room to room, trying to find something to occupy my mind and fill my time until Rebecca returned. I kept thinking about Jesus and all that Rebecca had told me about him. What would it be like to see him and hear his words?

All of a sudden, I knew. I must go to him.

Before I lost my courage, I quickly grabbed my shawl, threw it over my head, and hurried out the door.

My heart was pounding as I walked through the streets. What if someone saw me? Pulling the shawl closer to my face, I resolutely continued.

The breeze was cool as I left town and began walking down the rocky beach. A man was walking in front of me, obviously also in a hurry to get to Jesus. From the back, I could tell that he was very wealthy. His robe was rich and in the style of a priest. He must be from the synagogue. He hesitated for a moment and turned back toward me as if to see if anyone was following him. It was Jairus. He looked blankly at me; grief etched all over his face.

I stopped for a moment, fearful that he would recognize me. But he quickly turned around and continued walking down the beach. I breathed a sigh of relief.

I saw the crowds up ahead. They were watching a small boat coming ashore. A man was standing at the helm. He reached for the rope as they threw it to him, all the while laughing and talking with someone on the boat. I couldn't take my eyes off of him. He was medium height and obviously strong because of the way he grabbed the rope and pulled the boat to shore. There was a relaxed, easy way about him. He seemed unconcerned as the crowd began to press in toward the boat. This must be Jesus.

From a safe distance, I watched Jairus make his way through the crowd. Recognizing him, the crowd parted respectfully. As soon as Jesus stepped out of the boat onto the shore, Jairus knelt in front of him. The crowd was stunned, quietly falling back a bit allowing me to get a glimpse of Jairus and Jesus.

Forgetting myself, I drew closer to hear what was going on.

Jairus was pleading with Jesus. *"My little daughter is dying. Please come and put your hands on her so that she will be healed and live"* (Matthew 6:23 NIV).

Jesus reached out to Jairus and put his hand on his

arm to help him up. I didn't hear what he said but saw them start to walk together back toward where I was standing on the beach.

The crowd had grown. Word spread quickly that Jesus was going to Jairus' house. With my head bowed and my shawl clutched close to my face, I stood still as Jesus and the crowd passed me by. All of a sudden, out of nowhere, the thought came to me that if Jesus could heal the little girl, maybe he could heal me.

Before I lost my nerve, I hurried to catch up with Jesus. There was no way I would have the courage to speak to him. I would be horrified if people recognized me. Maybe if I could touch his cloak....

I made my way through the crowd, trying not to catch the eye of anyone I knew. The crowd stopped for a moment, and I had my chance. I edged my way forward just barely within reach of Jesus. Holding my breath, I timidly reached out and touched a tassel on the edge of his cloak.

It is difficult to explain what happened then. I felt a tingling start from the top of my head, flowing down into my heart and radiating throughout my body. The pain that I had endured for twelve years was simply gone. I placed my hand on my abdomen and felt only a rush of energy and well-being. I knew, without a doubt, that the bleeding had stopped. Wonder of wonders, I was healed.

In a daze, I heard Jesus say, *"Who touched me"* (Luke 8:45)? The disciple beside him said, *"Master, the people are crowding and pressing against you."*

Jesus began looking around. *"No, someone touched me; I know that power has gone out from me"* (Luke 8:46 NIV).

He continued to slowly pan the crowd until his

eyes met mine. Those piercing eyes looked into my very soul. Trembling, but no longer feeling any shame, I fell to my knees in front of him. My story began to pour out of me. Gently, he helped me to my feet. His eyes never left my face. Finally, he said tenderly, *"Daughter, your faith has healed you. Go in peace"* (Luke 8:48 NIV).

Joyfully, yet reluctantly, I turned to go. As I did, a group of men pushed through the crowd. They were from the house of Jairus. Sorrowfully, they walked up to him and said, "Your daughter is dead. There is no reason to bother the Teacher anymore."

Stricken, Jairus turned toward Jesus, his eyes pleading with him. Jesus told him, *"Don't be afraid; just believe"* (Luke 8:50 NIV).

Jesus instructed three of his followers to accompany him, and they followed Jairus back to town.

I knew that I must go to the synagogue to be cleansed, so I did not follow the crowd to Jairus' house. Later, I heard the story from Rebecca, of course.

Not knowing what happened to me, she burst into the house late that afternoon. "Leah, Leah. I have the most incredible news. Jairus' little daughter died, and Jesus brought her back to life!"

She stopped short when she saw me. "Leah, are you all right? You look different. What has happened to you?"

I hugged her and explained my wonderful news. "Rebecca, I too have been healed. I reached out and touched Jesus, and the power of God healed me through him.

She grabbed my hand and whispered hoarsely, "Leah, is this true? Sister, are you really healed?"

I nodded. "Yes, Rebecca, I am completely healed."

"Tell me what happened," Rebecca demanded.

"Tell me everything."

For the next hour, we sat together in the courtyard, laughing and crying as I told her all about my encounter with Jesus.

As dusk fell, Rebecca and I continued to sit quietly, thinking about the day. Breaking the silence, Rebecca asked, "Leah, do you think he is the One? Could he truly be the Messiah?"

"Yes, Sister. When I looked into his eyes, I knew that I saw God."

This was the first of many times that I told my incredible story. Of course, Rebecca also repeated it over and over to anyone who would listen. Years later, we were still telling our story of Jesus.

The Parable of the Workers in the Vineyard

Chapter Eleven

Matthew 20:1-16

I woke early to the annoying sound of the neighbor-hood rooster crowing loudly next door and my wife bringing in wood for the morning fire. My youngest, sprawled on his pallet on the other side of the room, sleepily asked me where I was going today.

"To work, Son."

At least, I hoped that I could find work today. There had been so many men in town looking for work during the harvest that I hadn't been able to hire on for very many days. Things were getting desperate, and I needed to make some money so that my wife could go to the market to buy food.

Walking to the center of the village, I could tell that it was going to be another warm and clear day. I met several men intent on the same purpose as I. We fell into step with each other, talking quietly of the coming day.

When we arrived, there were several hundred men ahead of us in line waiting to be hired. Discouraged, we lined up behind them, quietly thinking of those we left at home who were depending upon us to find work.

The first group of men were hired and left quickly to begin their day's work. We decided to stick around, hoping that more workers would be needed later in the morning.

The day was growing warm, causing us to grow drowsy. So, with little to discuss we propped up against a wall to wait. Around noon, the master came back for more laborers. We were still not chosen. By that time, I knew that I couldn't go back to face my family. I nodded off again in the warm sun.

I woke up with a start when I heard people talking excitedly around me. The master needed even more workers to finish the day's harvest. I figured that I wouldn't get much money, but a little was better than nothing at all.

We worked furiously for a couple of hours, and then it was quitting time already. Standing in line, I watched as the foreman handed out the pay for the day. Men around me began grumbling. The men who began work at noon were getting the same pay as the men who worked all day! I was dumbfounded. Did that mean that I might receive a little more than I had thought? To my astonishment, I received the same amount as the men who had worked all day.

Now there was a lot of complaining. One of the men who had worked all day was arguing angrily with the foreman.

"It is not fair that we who have worked all day receive the same pay as those who have only worked a couple of hours! Why do they get the same amount of money?"

The foreman said, "You agreed on that amount

when you started to work this morning. How could you begrudge the generosity of the master?"

As for me, I was very, very grateful for the day's wage. Now I could go home to face my family. Tomorrow my children would have a belly full of food, and tomorrow, I would go to work again and thank the master for his generosity.

Interlude Two

The Widow of Nain

Luke 7:12-15; 2 Kings 4:36

"Do not weep."
"But, Lord, he's dead!
My husband first and now my son."

"Do not weep."
"He's heavy, Lord.
The sun now sets, we must move on."

"Do not weep.
Young man, I say
to you , Arise."

The widow's son sat up
And spoke like Elijah's boy.
"Do not weep."

The Prostitute

Chapter Twelve

John 8:3-11

"Where are you going, woman?" he mumbled sleepily.

I had quietly slipped from the bed, thinking that he was asleep.

"I'm not finished with you yet."

"It is late," I said. "I must leave before the dawn. That was our agreement!"

Grumbling, he rolled over and turned his back to me. As I quickly dressed, I heard him snoring. Grateful for that, I snatched the coin from the table and quickly left the house.

Nervously looking around, I hurried down the street. Arriving at my house, I moved numbly, undressing and falling onto my pallet. I lay there trying to erase the memories of the night from my mind.

There were whispers about me in the town. The men would look slyly at me, and the women eyed me with scorn. I didn't care anymore. It was a very dangerous profession that I was in. I knew the penalty if I was caught, but it didn't matter.

It eventually happened—I knew it would. Two

nights later, I was caught. I did not see the men following me through the streets that night. They burst in on us early in the morning before I had a chance to sneak away. The men were Jewish leaders from the synagogue.

"Get up woman," one of them said scornfully. "Clothe yourself and come outside."

Resigned to my fate, I did as they said.

There was now a crowd of men waiting outside for me. I even recognized a couple of them, but of course, they would not make eye contact. They walked me to the synagogue.

It was market day, and the city had already begun to stir. People were taunting me as we paraded through the streets. I walked with my head down, covering my head and face with my scarf trying to block out the insults that were being thrown at me.

When we arrived at the synagogue, I glanced around and saw a group of men sitting in front of a man waving his hands and gesturing. Just another rabbi, I thought. We stood some distance away, and one of the Pharisees with me said loudly, "Teacher, may we speak to you?"

The man looked up and walked slowly toward us. As he did so, the Pharisee spoke loudly, *"Teacher, this woman was caught in the act of adultery! In the Law, Moses commanded us to stone such women. Now what do you say?"* (John 8:4,5 NIV).

My cheeks flamed and my heart pounded so loud that I thought surely someone would hear it in the silence that now permeated the courtyard.

The Pharisee then commanded of me, "Woman, kneel down!"

Slowly, I knelt and bowed my head. I heard the man

approaching. Then he did a very strange thing. He knelt beside me and began writing something in the dirt. Curious, I lifted my eyes to see what he was writing. Was it for my benefit, or was it for my accusers that he wrote, *God Forgives.* The men were not paying any attention to what he was writing, because they kept badgering him with questions about me and the Law. I knelt there, transfixed on those two words.

Finally, he straightened up, his glance catching mine as he did so. Very quietly he said, *"If any one of you is without sin, let him be the first to throw a stone at her"* (John 8:7 NIV). Then he stooped down again and began writing in the dirt. I braced myself for that stone.

All of a sudden, the questions ceased. Perhaps for the first time, the men stopped focusing on me and looked to see what Jesus had written. Quietly, the men began to slip away, the older ones first and then the younger ones until only Jesus and I were left.

Still stooped down, Jesus looked at me and smiled. His smile brought tears to my eyes. After a moment, he stood up and asked me, *"Woman, where are they? Has no one condemned you?"* (John 8:10 NIV).

"No one, Master," I replied, looking around at the now empty courtyard.

"Neither do I," he said. In a kind, yet firm voice, he continued. *"Go now and leave your life of sin"* (John 8:11 NIV). Gently, he took my hand and helped me to my feet.

I walked home in a daze, wondering what had happened. Who was this man who had saved my life? Most men I had encountered cared only for what they could get from me. This man protected me. For the first time in a long while, I felt clean on the inside.

What was I to do now? The town would not have

me, and I had no livelihood. My family had long ago deserted me. Perhaps I could join in with the men and women who followed Jesus.

And so, I did. There were three women who took me under their wings. They were Mary Magdalene, Joanna, and Susanna. Gratefully, I embraced this group as my very own family.

The Banquet

Chapter Thirteen

Luke 14:17-24

S o much excitement around the house. My master is giving a party, a wonderful, glorious party with a great banquet. It is a celebration. He wants to share his good news with friends and relatives.

He is a good man, caring and generous. With a huge smile, he tells me to invite many, many people. I carefully print out the invitation on a beautiful piece of papyrus and take it door to door.

Many of the guests that were invited said, "Of course, I will be there." Each was delighted with the invitation. So, my master was very pleased and looked forward to the grand evening.

Preparations took place all that week. On the last day, the cooks put the final touches on the bounteous banquet. My master called me about 5:00 in the evening.

"It is done. Go and tell the guests that everything is ready."

As I went from door to door to summon the guests, I couldn't believe what was happening. One by one, they began to tell me different excuses of why they could not come to the banquet that evening.

"I am so sorry, but I bought a piece of land today, and I must go and see it."

"I purchased five yokes of oxen, and I am on my way to the field to test them."

"Sir, I eloped this very afternoon. You must understand why I cannot come."

One by one I heard their excuses. What will my master say? I know how disappointed he will be. All that food; all the preparations.

When I got back to the house to tell him, he angrily replied, "None of those men will taste my supper. Go out quickly to the street corners, to the homeless, to the maimed, the blind, and the lame. Invite them to my house for the banquet of their lives."

And so, I did. At first, they did not believe me.

"You are inviting me to a banquet?"

"You must be tricking me."

"I am blind, can you lead me to the master so that I might taste of the good food?"

"The master's house, you say? I can hardly believe my good fortune."

These men were filled with joy and excitement, and yes, thanksgiving.

When they came to the mansion, there was room for even more, so the master sent me out past the city to the highways and under the bridges.

"Tell them to come! The master has provided so much food, drink, and fun."

What a night that was. Those poor people, who had nothing, enjoyed a banquet like they had never experienced in their entire lives.

This pleased my master.

The Ten Lepers

Chapter Fourteen

Luke 17:11-19

It is so hot. I feel the searing sun beating down on the top of my head, accentuating the pain that is shooting through my neck and down into my back. At least there is feeling there. My fingers and toes have lost all sensation, destroyed by the terrible disease that has eaten away at my body and into my very soul.

We must sit here and wait, they say. The Master often travels this road on his way into the city. We heard about him healing people, even raising some from the dead. Do we dare hope?

What a pitiful group we are, ten outcasts with no one to take care of us. No one cares about us; even my family cannot bear the sight of me. We are bonded together by our infirmity, an unusual group with religious differences forgotten. They have even quit harassing me about being a Samaritan. It just doesn't matter.

We heard him coming before we caught a glance of him. There was a low murmur that grew louder as he approached the village. I, being the youngest in the group, dared to venture a little closer to see if I could spot him. The others were too afraid of being stoned by the villagers. There he was! I hobbled back to gather up the group. We shuffled as close as we dared, one mass of ragged, sick, putrid humanity.

The crowd eyed us fearfully as we approached. One member of our group dared to speak, *"Master, have mercy on us!"*

Gathering courage several others of us chimed in, *"Jesus, Master, have mercy on us"* (Luke 17:13)!

Amid the clamor, he looked our way. Even from that distance, I felt his eyes on me. A warm feeling came over me. It started in my chest and began radiating out to my disfigured fingers and toes. Startled, I looked down at my hands. I hadn't felt any sensation in them for several years.

He walked over closer to us, a look of concern on his face. We stood there, mesmerized by his presence. *"Go, show yourselves to the priests"* (Luke 17:14 NLT).

We looked at each other doubtfully. We must be clean to show ourselves to the priests. At first, we did not even move, but just looked at him dumbly. Did we dare? I glanced around at the other nine men and then back at Jesus. Resolutely, I said, "We must go." It took an act of will to turn my back on him and walk toward the synagogue. Surprisingly, the other men followed me.

We walked slowly at first, aware of his eyes on us. When we were out of his sight, we tried to walk a little faster. As my stride increased, I begin to feel a cool, tingling sensation spreading from the top of my head, down over my disfigured ears, down my neck, and radiating throughout my body. Looking around at the others, I could tell something was happening to them, too. Our pace quickened, and we began to run, an ecstatic, ragtag group flapping our arms and shouting to the heavens. We didn't stop running until we arrived at the steps of the synagogue. Flopping down on the steps, we spread our hands and feet in front of us and stared at them in disbelief. In place of the burned stubs that used to be our fingers and toes, were beautiful pink appendages.

The priest came outside when he heard our commotion. What a sight we must have been, ten lepers dressed in filthy rags, rejoicing as if we were drunk. Staying at a safe distance, he asked what we were doing at the synagogue.

We all shouted, "We are healed. The Master has healed our leprosy."

Still sitting on the steps, like proud little children we held up our restored hands and feet. Seeing that this was indeed true, he allowed us to enter the synagogue to be cleansed.

All that is, except me. I am a Samaritan, and I could not enter the synagogue. I waited for them on the steps.

When they walked out of the synagogue an hour later, they were free men, free from disease and fear. They talked excitedly about going home to their families. They had already forgotten the Master. But I couldn't forget the look in the man's eyes that not only healed my body but also touched that place in my spirit that had been empty for so long.

I stood up when they appeared and said, "We must go back and thank the Master." They looked at each other and then at me.

"Yes, you go and thank him for us. We are going to our homes."

At that, all nine turned and walked down the synagogue steps and off in different directions, leaving me standing there.

Undaunted, I left to look for Jesus. I found him sitting with a group of his followers. I approached timidly, still unsure of my status in society. He looked up and smiled at me. At that smile, forgetting all else, I ran toward him shouting, "Praise God, I'm healed!" Reaching him, I fell to my knees at his feet.

He reached down and touched my shoulder. "Where are your friends?"

Jesus looked around at his disciples. *"Were there not ten cleansed? But where are the nine? Were there not any found who returned to give glory to God except this foreigner?"* He patted my shoulder and said, *"Arise, go your way. Your faith has made you well"* (Luke 17:17, 18).

At that point, I knew my healing was complete, not only from leprosy but from years of pain and rejection. Jesus healed the emptiness of my life.

Unfortunately, my other nine friends did not come back to complete their healing—the healing of the spirit and soul.

The Woman at the Well

Chapter Fifteen

John 4

It is the noon hour, and I am quietly making my way through the silent streets, my water jar balanced on top of my head. A trickle of sweat drips down into my right eye, and I wipe it away. It is unbearably hot. My feet burn from the heat radiating from the ground through the thin leather of my sandals.

It is always quiet at noon because that is when people retreat into their houses to rest and escape the heat. I am not trying to escape the heat; I am trying to escape the women. The last time I went to the well in the evening, I promised myself that I would never go at that time of day again. The women were so hateful, rolling their eyes and then turning away. What a gossipy bunch, filling their husbands' ears with all kinds of stories about me. So now is the best time for me to go and draw water. We have no more water in the house, so I have no choice. I will simply go when no one else is there, draw my water, and leave peacefully. Surely no one will be at the well in the heat of the day to bother me.

After arriving at the well, I am so busy going about my task that I am startled when I hear a man's voice ask me, "May I have a drink, please?" I look up quickly, wondering who would even be talking to me, much less asking me for a drink.

It is a Jewish rabbi. Of all things—a Jewish rabbi asking a Samaritan woman for a drink. I said as much to him. He smiled and shook his head at me. There was something very unusual about him. He stood there in front of me, quietly waiting. I looked at him suspiciously as I reached down and pulled the bucket out of the water.

Then he said the strangest thing to me.

"If you knew the gift of God, and who it is who says to you, 'Give Me a drink,' you would have asked Him, and He would have given you living water."

That made no sense to me. *"Sir, you have nothing to draw with, and the well is deep. Where then do you get that living water? Are you greater than our father, Jacob, who gave us the well, and drank from it himself, as well as his sons and his livestock?"*

I still cannot believe that I am standing here talking to this Jewish man. Who in the world is he? Why would he be talking to me, a Samaritan woman? And what is this Living Water that he is talking about?

Something is stirring in me as we speak. I have never had such a conversation with a man. It is forbidden for a woman to even speak to a rabbi; how much more for me, a Samaritan woman, considered an outcast by the Jews.

As if reading my thoughts, the man said, *"Whoever drinks of the water that I shall give him will never thirst. But the water that I shall give him will become in him a fountain of water springing up into everlasting life."*

Almost jokingly I said, *"Sir, give me this water, that I may not thirst, nor come here to draw."* It would be nice not to have to face the village women again, I thought to myself.

He smiled at me and said, "Go, call your husband and come here."

I turned my head away and whispered, "I have no husband."

He looked at me intently, but with no accusation in his voice said, *"You have well said, 'I have no husband,' for you have had five husbands, and the one whom you now have is not your husband; in that, you spoke truly."*

I looked back at him in surprise and a little fear. How in the world did he know these things? What kind of man am I speaking to? He must be a prophet—a holy man. Maybe I could presume to ask him a question.

"Sir, our fathers worshiped on this mountain, and you Jews say that in Jerusalem is the place where one ought to worship. Where do we worship God?"

He told me that the hour was coming when God will not be worshiped on this mountain or in Jerusalem, but God will be worshiped in Spirit and Truth because God is Spirit.

It was so very quiet, the only sound, the drone of one little insect, circling my bucket, trying desperately to get a drink. I stared at it, thinking about what he was saying to me.

Slowly, I looked into his face and said very cautiously, *"I know that the Messiah is coming. When he comes, he will tell us all things."*

Then he said something that changed my life forever. As he looked deep within my soul, he said, *"I who speak to you am he."*

Startled, I drew in a deep breath and stepped back away from him, suddenly weak from an overwhelming sense of love that flowed through me. I stared at him, mesmerized by the very presence of him. I knew—at that moment, I knew what he said was true.

I didn't even notice his disciples walking up behind us until I heard someone clear his throat. Reluctantly, I looked around to see four men standing behind the well looking very embarrassed because their master was speaking to me. I glanced back at the man, and he was smiling at all of us.

"My friends, come—come have a drink of cool water that this woman has drawn for us!"

Shaking myself I quickly left the man and his friends, my precious water jar forgotten in my haste to get away. At that moment all I cared about was telling someone what had just happened to me. They must be told that I have met the Messiah!

The town was beginning to wake from its midday nap. Calling to each person as I ran through the town, I was laughing and crying at the same time. *"Come see a Man who has told me everything that I have ever done!"*

"Where is this man?" Over and over, they asked the question.

"He's at the well. The Messiah is at the well!"

A group of the villagers found the Teacher at the well and urged Him to stay longer in the village. We could not believe that a Jewish man would stay in a village of Samaritans. What a wonderful gift was given to us.

One cool evening after He had left, I timidly made my way back to the well. This time the women greeted me with smiles. What a difference this man, Jesus, had made in our lives.

As we drew the sweet water from Jacob's well, they said, *"Now we believe, not because of what you said, for we have heard Him, and we know that this is indeed the Christ, the Savior of the world."*

The Blind Man

Chapter Sixteen

Luke 18:35-43; Matthew 20:29-34; Mark 10:46-52

I am blind. I don't ever remember seeing. I was told that as a child I could see a little, but the images are blurred in my mind, too far back in time. I spend my days alongside the road to Jericho. This is a very busy road, a good place to sit and beg for the few coins that people choose to throw my way. For the most part, they ignore me, walking along the road, hurrying to get to their destinations.

Others sit and beg beside me. Sometimes we talk to pass the time. Lately the talk is of the man, Jesus. Some say he is a prophet, even Elijah back from the dead. Some say he is a blasphemer—claiming, of all things, to be God. We have even heard that he has healed the sick and raised the dead. I shake my head when I hear of these things.

One day as I was sitting up against a scruffy tree in my usual spot, I heard a commotion. It was loud as if many people—a multitude—were walking down the road. The wind was out of the south, so I could smell the dust in the air and taste it in my mouth. I quickly put my arm up to my nose and mouth to block out the dust. From the sound of the voices and the thud of the feet,

I could tell there were a lot of people. What was happening? I called out to whoever was closest. "What does this mean? What is going on?" The noise grew louder as the crowd approached. People were all around me now, jostling and pushing. Again, I called out to someone—anyone. "It's the man, Jesus," someone said. "Jesus of Nazareth is passing by."

I stumbled to my feet, grasping at the air, wondering where he was. My heart started pounding in my chest as I turned this way and that—my arms outstretched. People began shoving me as they walked by, unmindful of my fear. Without thinking, I cried out, *"Jesus, Son of David, have mercy on me!"* My voice was loud carrying above the noise of the crowd. I cried out again, even louder this time. *"Son of David, have mercy on me!"* I could feel his presence in this crowd. Frantically, I cried out again. I could not let him leave me.

I continued to cry out for him, ignoring the people around me who were telling me to be quiet and sit down. Finally, I felt a hand on my arm and heard a kind voice in my ear saying, "It's all right, he wants you to come to him."

I sensed that the crowd parted for me as I was led to Jesus. Feeling his presence, his peace, his power—I automatically reached out my hands in front of me as if to touch him. He asked me, *"What do you want Me to do for you?"*

I replied, *"Lord, that I may receive my sight."* There was a hush in the crowd now. I could almost feel their eyes on us.

Jesus said to me, *"Receive your sight. Your faith has made you well."* Immediately the darkness turned to light. I reached for my eyes, protecting them from the brightness. And then slowly, as I lowered my hands, I could see his face with the kindest, most compassionate eyes looking back at me. I could see! I could see! I shouted, "Praise God, I can see!" Immediately the crowd began laughing, shouting, and praising God with me. The word was passed back through the crowd. "The blind man—the beggar of Jericho, he can see."

I turned back to Jesus; he was smiling—a smile that lit up his face. He put out his hand and grasped my shoulder and said, "Come, my friend, we're going to Jericho!"

Joyfully, I joined the crowd and followed Jesus down the road (Mark 10:52 NIV).

Zacchaeus

Chapter Seventeen

Luke 19:1-10

Stories have been flying all around the town about the healing of the blind man of Jericho. I have seen him sitting along the road, day in and day out. Sometimes I have thrown him a few coins, not paying him much mind. Now they say he has been healed.

My name is Zacchaeus, and I am the chief tax collector in Jericho. I may not be very popular with the people, but my earnings are excellent. As long as I am making money, I am happy. At least, I think I am.

One day I was talking to my friend, Thaddeus. "That man, Jesus," my friend was telling me, "all kinds of things happen when he is around."

I looked at him, shaking my head and laughing. "I must meet this man," I replied.

Several days later my wish came true. I was sitting at my stall, looking over my figures and noting that several people in the district still owed money on their taxes. Interrupting my train of thought, Thaddeus ran up to tell me that Jesus was coming this way.

There is always a huge entourage with this man, so I knew it would be impossible for me to even get a glimpse of Jesus. I am very short in stature and find it very frustrating to be in the middle of a crowd, straining on tiptoe, looking to one side or another over the shoulders of people in front of me.

Knowing the route that he would take through town, I remembered a sycamore tree on the way. I hurriedly took a shortcut through several streets, running as fast as my short legs would take me. Arriving at the tree, I quickly climbed up into its branches and settled down to wait. Several people walked by, looking at me with amusement. I know they were wondering what on earth the chief tax collector was doing up in that sycamore tree.

Soon I heard a low murmur as the crowd approached. I had only hoped to get a better glimpse of Jesus, so I was astonished when he stopped under the tree and looked up at me. With undeniable humor in his voice and a smile on his face, he called my name. "Zacchaeus!" he said. "Quick, come down! I must be a guest in your home today"

"My house, Lord?" I said with surprise.

"Yes, your house, Zacchaeus," Jesus answered.

As I quickly scrambled down the tree, I thought to myself, how in the world did he know my name? Down on the ground, I tried to straighten my clothes the best I could. Then, looking up at Jesus (for he was much taller than I), I said with as much dignity as I could muster, "It will be a pleasure, Lord."

The crowd heard this exchange between Jesus and me. To my right, I heard someone say, "Can you believe it? Jesus is going to Zacchaeus' house to stay. Does Jesus not know that Zacchaeus is a tax collector and a sinner?"

Ignoring the murmuring around me, I glanced up

at Jesus and felt something begin to happen in my spirit. Standing there in front of Jesus and the crowd, I promised, *"Look, Lord, I give half of my goods to the poor; and if I have taken anything from anyone by false accusation, I restore fourfold"* (Luke 19:8).

Jesus looked directly at me and said firmly and loud enough for those around us to hear, *"Today salvation has come to this house, because this man, too, is a son of Abraham. For the Son of Man came to seek and to save what was lost"* (Luke 19:9 NIV).

Interlude Three

The Pearl of Great Price
Matthew 13:45, 46

I am a merchant; I deal in jewels.

My jewels are for women,

Some young and some old.

My jewelry is deceptively beautiful and –

Not always real.

One day, however, I came across a pearl—

An incredibly exquisite jewel.

A pearl pulled from the pain of an oyster.

Growing slowly--buffered

A seed that is so deep that it hurts.

But through the pain came

An incredibly beautiful jewel.

A pearl of great price.

But how? What sacrifice? Nothing matters

But that I sell all I have

To get this Jewel.

The Woman from Syria Phoenicia

Chapter Eighteen

Matthew 15:21-28; Mark 7:24-30

In the land of Zebulun and of Naphtali,
beside the sea, beyond the Jordan River—
in Galilee where so many Gentiles live—
the people who sat in darkness
have seen a great light.
And for those who lived in the land
where death casts its shadow,
a light has shined.
—Matthew 4:15, 16 (NLT)

T he water of the Mediterranean was exquisite, blue against an azure sky. The sun felt warm on my face, contrasting to the cool spray of the ocean waves. It was a perfect day; we did not have many days like this. I watched as my little seven-year-old ran toward the water. She was so beautiful and innocent. Her shiny black hair was flying behind her as she ran along the water's edge, skipping through the waves, laughing and shouting, "Mama, come run with me! Come and run with me!" Right at her heels was her beloved dog, Rome, nipping at her heels, barking and splashing. I couldn't help it—I gathered up my skirts and joined the chase, a child myself, once again.

I caught up with Ami, gathered her up in my arms, and swung her around giggling and squirming until we both fell in a heap on the sand. Rome pounced on top of us, tail wagging and panting. Before he could lick our faces, I pushed him back and sat up. "Rome, go away!" Exhausted, Ami and I sat there in the sand, digging our toes into its warm dampness, totally content.

Our days were not always like this. I never knew when my little girl might suddenly, during her play, grab her head and start screaming hysterically, shouting to an unknown demon in or around her. I would try to hold on to her during these fits, but she would scratch or bite me until I would have to let her go. Even at night she sometimes would wake, moaning and crying until I would go to her and try to calm her down.

Everyone in town avoids us now, fearful of this beautiful child. That is why I bring her to the beach to play. Ami seems calmer beside the sea, free to be a little child, to run and shout, to dig in the sand. Her only friend is her dog, Rome. She found him one day hurt and limping, wandering down this very beach. He is ferociously loyal to her and is always close by, even when she is having one of her fits.

"Ami, we must go home now. Perhaps your father will return home today."

Ami's eyes lit up, and she jumped to her feet, gathering the little bowls that she had brought to the beach. Her small hand in mine, she chattered happily as we made our way home.

My husband, Alton, is a merchant who deals in

delicate and exquisite textiles. He goes often to the wharf in Tyre where the huge and majestic Roman and Greek ships sail in with his goods. He then must travel, taking his beautiful fabrics as far south as Jerusalem. Any day now he will return from such a journey. He has been gone for two months, and we are anxious to see him. Alton is a hardworking man, very dedicated to Ami and me. She is our only child, and she adores her father.

Much to our delight, Alton was home when we arrived. Ami giggled as he lifted her above his head and swung her around in a circle.

Alton always has many stories to share after one of his journeys; Ami and I love to hear these tales. That evening, we sat around the table and listened as he told us about some of the places where he had been and the people that he had met. As always, Rome sat at Ami's feet underneath the table, waiting for a small tidbit of her meal to fall to the floor. She loved to sneak him something when she thought her father wasn't looking. Later, Ami climbed on her father's lap and fell asleep in his arms, exhausted by her day at the beach. Alton and I continued to talk quietly late into the night.

"Tell me about Ami. How has she been since I have been gone?" he whispered.

"The demon has troubled her many times," I answered softly.

We both sat there in silence for several minutes, looking at Ami's sweet face and listening to her quiet and rhythmic breathing.

Finally, Alton looked back at me and spoke hesitantly. "On my journey, I have seen a miracle worker from Galilee. Perhaps . . . " His voice trailed off.

I knew what he was thinking. A miracle—we

needed a miracle.

Alton hesitated and then continued, "But, he is a Jew; I do not know if he will have anything to do with us." I nodded in agreement. "Yes, they hate us. It is said that their god destroyed our beautiful city and the island city across the bay, making Tyre an uninhabited ruin. Once we were even greater than we are now until Nebuchadnezzar came with his army to plunder and destroy us. The Jewish prophet foretold it:

'O famous island city,
once ruler of the sea,
how you have been destroyed!
Your people, with their naval power,
once spread fear around the world.
Now the coastlands tremble at your fall.
The islands are dismayed as you pass away'" (Ezekiel 26:17, 18 NLT).

We both looked at Ami. Alton spoke again, "But this man seems to be different than the other Jews." Alton stopped speaking, closed his eyes, and bowed his head. I sensed that he had more to say about the man. I touched him gently on the arm and said, "Tell me about this miracle worker. What is his name?" I asked.

"He is called Jesus of Nazareth."

"Where did you see him?"

"In my travels these last few months, the talk was of nothing else. They spoke of him in Jerusalem and Galilee. As I was traveling through Galilee last month, people were coming from all over to hear him preach and to bring their sick to him. I had heard so much about him that I decided to stop my journey and listen to him preach."

"What did he say to the people?"

"He spoke of the Kingdom of Heaven."

"The Kingdom of Heaven?"

I saw something in Alton's eyes that I had never seen before. Was it joy? Was it hope? I smiled at him and urged him to continue his story.

"He told us these parables: *'The Kingdom of Heaven is like a treasure that a man discovered hidden in a field. In his excitement, he hid it again and sold everything he owned to get enough money to buy the field—and to get the treasure, too!'* (Matthew 13:44 NLT).

'Again, the Kingdom of Heaven is like a pearl merchant on the lookout for choice pearls. When he discovered a pearl of great value, he sold everything he owned and bought it!'" (Matthew 13:45, 46 NLT).

I laughed and replied, "I would like to live in that kingdom."

Alton nodded his head and said, "He also encouraged people to keep on asking for what they needed from God. He said, *'Keep on asking, and you will be given what you ask for. Keep on looking, and you will find. Keep on knocking, and the door will be opened. For everyone who asks, receives. Everyone who seeks, finds'"* (Matthew 7:7, 8 NLT).

"Everyone?" I interrupted.

"He said that the door was open to everyone who knocks on it. He then spoke to those of us who are parents. *'You parents——if your children ask for a loaf of bread, do you give them a stone instead? Or if they ask for a fish, do you give them a snake?'"* (Matthew 7:9, 10 NLT).

I shook my head in dismay at the thought and blurted out, "Of course not!"

Alton smiled at me. "That's exactly what the preacher said. The man's voice became very quiet, and I had to strain to hear, but I think I heard him say, *'If you sinful people know how to give good gifts to your children, how much more will your heavenly Father give good gifts to those who ask him'"* (Matthew 7:11 NLT).

We both looked at Ami. Alton picked her up gently and laid her in her bed. Rome padded close behind, curling up at the foot of her pallet.

"Do you think the miracle worker could help Ami?" I asked.

"I don't know," he said honestly, "but we must do something."

The next morning, I was sweeping our small little house when I heard Rome start to bark. He only did that when Ami was beginning one of her fits. Perhaps it is the demon that taunts even the dog. I hurried outside to see Ami curled in a ball moaning. Rome was standing over her growling at some unknown entity. I knew it would get worse, so I gathered her up in my arms and quickly brought her inside. Suddenly, she began scratching and clawing me, moaning and crying out. The moans turned to shrieks until the room echoed with them. I could only stand by helplessly as Ami fell to the floor, writhing and screaming.

Abruptly, and without warning, Ami's little body relaxed, limp as if she were dead. The silence was as eerie as the horrible shrieks and cries had been a few minutes earlier. I knew that she would now sleep deeply for many hours on end, so still that she would hardly seem to even breathe. I held her in my arms, rocking back and forth, back and forth, praying that some god would take this demon from her.

Suddenly, an idea began to build within me. I thought about the conversation that Alton and I had last night when he spoke about the miracle worker. I would find that man from Galilee. I didn't know how, but I would find him. I would do anything to rid my precious child of this demon. I fell asleep that night, holding Ami close to my heart, a small seed of hope beginning to grow within me.

Several weeks later, Alton came home from the wharf with amazing news.

"I have heard that the miracle worker from Galilee has come to Tyre. A merchant friend of mine knows where Jesus is staying. He is with his disciples; they have come to Tyre to get away from the crowds in Galilee and Jerusalem."

I looked at him and said, "Alton, you must stay with Ami. I am going to find Jesus and bring him here to heal her."

Alton frowned at me and said, "I'm not sure that this Jewish man will have anything to do with gentiles. I do not want you to be disappointed."

I shook my head. "I must at least try. Remember, he said to keep on asking, keep on looking, and keep on knocking. Ami is depending on us. Please tell me where I can find him."

The town was quiet, settling down for the evening as I made my way through the narrow streets. I usually loved this time of day when the evening brought a cool breeze from the sea. Merchants were putting away their wares, women with water jugs balanced on their heads were hurrying home, and children were playing in the streets. I passed a beautiful little girl about Ami's age sitting outside the door of her home playing quietly with a fat little puppy. She was giggling as the puppy chased after its tail. My thoughts returned to Ami, and I quickened my pace.

I almost lost my courage when I stopped in front of the house where Jesus was supposed to be staying. I was sweating by this time and felt thankful for a fresh breeze blowing softly from the sea. Nervously, I licked my lips, tasting the salt in the air. I heard voices coming from the courtyard, so, taking a deep breath, I knocked on the door. No one answered, and I knocked again. There was still no answer. This time I pushed the gate to the courtyard open and walked in.

I spotted him immediately. He was sitting on a bench surrounded by a small group of men. They were laughing and talking, as men will do, paying no attention to me. What should I do? Walk up to him and just start talking? How could I ever get his attention? Then I remembered Ami, her precious face contorted in agony as the demon tormented her.

Without thinking, I cried out, *"Have mercy on me, O Lord, Son of David! My daughter is severely demon-possessed"* (Matthew 15:22)!

He looked toward me but said nothing.

Remembering what Alton had told me "to keep on asking," I ran to Jesus and kneeled at his feet repeating over and over, *"Lord, cast the demon out of my daughter!"*

Above my head, I heard his friends say, "Lord, you have come to Tyre to get away from this. Send her away, her cries are annoying."

Undeterred, I continued to cry out until I heard him say softly, *"I was not sent except to the lost sheep of the house of Israel"* (Matthew 15:24).

Still kneeling, I looked up and said tearfully, "Lord, help me" (Matthew 15:25)!

Jesus spoke to me and said not unkindly, *"Let the children be filled first, for it is not good to take the children's*

TO SEE HIM FACE TO FACE

bread and throw it to the little dogs" (Mark 7:27).

Thinking of Rome and how he would sit patiently and wait for Ami to slip him a tidbit under the table, I said, "*Yes, Lord, yet even the little dogs under the table eat from the children's crumbs*" (Mark 7:28)!

He smiled at me, his eyes crinkling with kindness and good humor. Reaching down to help me up, he said, "*O woman, great is your faith. Let it be to you as you desire. For this saying go your way; the demon has gone out of your daughter*" (Matthew 15:28; Mark 7:29).

Stunned, I backed away from him. Who was this man to heal my daughter from afar? The men with him were quiet and embarrassed, glancing at him and then at me. Finally, I turned to leave, hesitant and still not sure I had heard him correctly. I stopped at the gate of the courtyard and turned around one more time. The men had continued their conversation with each other, but Jesus looked toward me and smiled. Our eyes met, and an incredible joy welled up inside of me. I knew from that moment that I would never be the same again. Reluctantly, I left his presence and began to run toward home and Ami. Could it be true? Was the demon truly gone?

It was dark when I finally arrived home. I entered quietly, thinking Ami might already be asleep. I was surprised and delighted to find Ami awake and lying quietly on her pallet. Alton was sitting nearby. Ami's sweet face lit up when she saw me walk into the room. She sat up on her bed and said, "Mama, it's gone, it's gone!" Alton was grinning from ear to ear also.

"What do you mean, Ami?" I asked, kneeling at her eye level.

"The bad demon is gone from me. I saw it leave my head."

Not fully understanding all that had happened, I asked Alton to explain.

"It is true. This evening after you left, Rome began barking like he does when the demon begins to torment Ami. Suddenly, she grabbed her head and stood up. Her hands then flew from her head, and Rome ran out the door like he was chasing something. She told me that the demon had left her head."

I wrapped my arms around her and said, "Yes, I know that the demon is gone from you. Jesus told it to go. It will never bother you again."

After Ami went to sleep, Alton and I talked late into the night. I told him all about my meeting with Jesus.

"I will take you to the house tomorrow," I promised.

"Yes, we must go back and thank Jesus."

The next day, Alton, Ami, and I arrived at the house where Jesus was staying. After knocking repeatedly on the door, a man came and told us that Jesus was no longer there. He and his friends had gone back to Galilee.

Disappointed, we walked slowly back home.

"We will find him again," Alton promised.

I could only nod, thinking of the man who had changed our lives forever.

Squeezing Ami's hand, I nodded and said, "Yes, we will find him again."

*****

Years later, it was Ami's turn to go out and seek Him. This time she met the risen Christ and became a follower of "The Way". The man who healed her and cast out the demon from her became her Savior and Lord. Ami shared with her father and me that "there is no difference between Jew and Gentile—the same Lord is Lord of all and richly blesses all who calls on him, for, *"everyone who calls on the name of the Lord will be saved"* (Romans 10:12,13 NIV). She led us to Christ, and we were finally able to thank Jesus for healing our child.

Amen.

If you confess with your mouth, "Jesus is Lord", and believe in your heart that God raised him from the dead, you will be saved (Romans 10:9 NIV).

Mary and Martha

Chapter Nineteen

Luke 10:38-42; John 11:1-46; John 12:1-8;
Mathew. 26:6-13; Mark 14:3-9

"**M**ary, hurry, we must go." Martha called impatiently to me as she rushed out the door. Martha was always in a hurry and would get very annoyed with me if I dawdled. We were on our way to the market. Martha always wanted to get there early to beat the crowd and pick the best produce.

Jesus was coming to our house for supper, and Martha wanted it to be perfect for him. This was not the first time that Jesus and his disciples had eaten supper with us. We had met Jesus when our brother Lazarus brought him home for supper several months ago.

Lazarus had been in Jerusalem on business that day. Visiting the temple before he came home, he noticed Jesus in a heated discussion with several religious leaders. Lazarus was intrigued that someone dared argue with the Pharisees. He had heard all about this teacher. People all over Jerusalem were talking about him. Some called Jesus a prophet, some a miracle worker, others called him a fake. But there were also whispers that he might be the Messiah. Walking up to Jesus, Lazarus invited him to come to our house for supper. We became very good friends after that.

We had many wonderful conversations around the dinner table. One evening, I asked Jesus so many questions that Martha, embarrassed for me, broke in and apologized to Jesus for my impudence. He smiled at Martha and assured her that I was not out of line at all. I was so hungry for what Jesus had to say. As time went on, I began to believe that maybe he was the Messiah.

Martha and I finished our shopping quickly because we had so many preparations to attend to before he arrived. Martha had a long list of chores that must be done before supper that evening. She fussed at me if I dawdled, my thoughts often drifting to Jesus. I loved creating questions in my mind that I intended to ask him the next time he came to visit. My list of questions was getting to be as long as Martha's list of chores.

We were hosting a special dinner tonight because Jesus was leaving Jerusalem for a while. I think the situation with the religious leaders was heating up, and he needed to get away. Lazarus said he was going over to the other side of the Jordan, the place where he was baptized.

Finally, the evening was here, and Jesus and his disciples arrived. How can I explain how I felt when I saw him? I was in awe of him, yet comfortable at the same time. He was such a wonderful guest, making those around him feel alive and full of joy.

Lazarus and Jesus entered into an easy conversation. They had become very close friends. My brother has such a quick laugh, and it would ring through the house whenever he and Jesus were together. Lazarus always had a funny story to tell, and he would have Jesus laughing in no time. I have seen Jesus laughing so hard that tears rolled down his face over one of Lazarus' funny tales. Our home was a sanctuary to Jesus, a place to relax and recharge. Lazarus made sure of it.

Martha and I greeted the guests, and she quickly excused herself to go to the kitchen to finish preparations for the evening meal. I intended to follow her but got caught up in the conversation between Jesus, Lazarus, and the other disciples. I was fascinated with the stories I heard, and I tried very hard to sit quietly by and just listen—but I couldn't do it. Questions began to bubble out of me, and I found myself entering into the conversation. My brother, understanding my unquenchable thirst for knowledge, looked at me in amusement. Jesus listened to me and responded as if I were a man of equal stature.

My revelry was broken, however, when Martha walked back into the room, a frown on her face. She looked at me but addressed Jesus. *"Lord, do you not care that my sister has left me to serve alone? Tell her to get up and help me"* (Luke 10:40).

Embarrassed, I scrambled to my feet. As I did so, I heard Jesus say, *"Martha, Martha, you work too hard and worry too much. One thing is important, and Mary has chosen it. It will not be taken from her."*

Martha stood for a moment, bowed her head, and then returned to the kitchen. I followed after her, not sure if she was angry or not. Surprisingly, when I got to the kitchen, she simply gave me a stack of dishes and asked quietly if I would set the table for her, with no mention of what just happened.

How can I explain Martha? She is a wonderful sister, down to earth and ever so practical. Her mind is on basic things like cooking, cleaning, and running the household. She serves God by simply doing that—serving. Martha is always giving—to Lazarus, to me, to others —but she never allows anyone to give to her. This is noble to a point, but I sense that sometimes she is a bit resentful. She tries to hide it, but we all know that when she is like that, we need to stay out of her way.

The evening went well after that. Martha finally relaxed and started enjoying herself. After the guests had left, we began talking.

"Mary, who do you think Jesus really is?"

"He is our friend," I said.

"Yes, of course," she replied. "But he is more than that, isn't he?"

Several days later, Lazarus came home feeling ill. At first, we thought nothing of it, sending him to bed with a cool rag for his head and a bowl of Martha's delicious fish soup. But as the night drew on, his fever began to rise, and we could not get it to come down. We worked throughout the night, but by morning, he was desperately ill. How could someone go from being so perfectly well and strong to this?

"Mary!" Martha called to me from out in the courtyard. I was trying to spoon some water into Lazarus' mouth and reluctantly left his bedside to see what she wanted.

"We must find Jesus," Martha whispered to me.

There was fear in her eyes, and yet when she said Jesus' name, we both felt a strange peace.

"Yes, Martha," I said confidently. "He will come immediately and heal Lazarus. He has gone over to the other side of the Jordan. We will send a servant to find him."

I quickly summoned a servant and said, "Please, go and find Jesus. When you find him, tell him this: '*Lord, be-*

hold, he whom You love is sick'" (John 11:3).

When the servant came back the next day, Martha and I quickly ran out to meet him. Anxiously, I blurted out, "Did you find him? Did you find Jesus?"

"Yes, I found Jesus and his followers."

"What did he say? Is he coming?" I asked impatiently.

"He said that this sickness is not fatal. It will become an occasion to show God's glory by glorifying God's Son."

Martha and I were stunned. What did this mean?

Our servant looked at both of us, bowed his head, and said quietly, "Jesus did not follow me."

*****

Lazarus died that night.

Martha and I walked through the house in a daze, taking care of the mundane details that had to be attended to after someone has died. We prepared his body, lovingly anointing Lazarus with spices and wrapping him in the beautiful burial cloth. With tears rolling down our faces, we watched the servants lift Lazarus and carry him to the family tomb. The mourners were waiting as the stone was rolled across the grave. Our precious, loving brother was gone. Martha and I sent the mourners away, and we sat beside the stone, too numb to cry anymore.

I looked at Martha after a long period of silence. "Martha?"

"Yes, Mary?"

"Why did Jesus not come? Why did he let us down? He loves us. He could have healed Lazarus like he healed the others." The questions that were smothering my heart finally started pouring out.

Martha shook her head. "I don't know why. I have no answers for you." She came over to me and we hugged, holding on to each other because we felt God had surely abandoned us.

Three days later, Martha and I were in the kitchen helping to serve the many guests who still came by to give their condolences. We heard a commotion outside. Immediately, a servant rushed to the door to tell us that Jesus and his disciples were on the outskirts of Bethany and coming this way.

Martha turned to look at me. She grabbed my hand and said, "Mary, we must go and greet him."

"I can't, Martha," I pleaded. "I can't face him."

Martha squeezed my hand, removed her apron, threw her scarf over her head, and went to meet Jesus.

As Martha walked to the edge of town, all of her questions, doubts, and fears threatened to overwhelm her practical mind. What would she say to Jesus when she saw him? What would be his explanation for letting them down?

Seeing Jesus walking toward her, Martha blurted out, tears streaming down her face, *"Lord if You had been here, my brother would not have died."* She stopped short as if realizing the sharpness of her words. Bowing her head to hide her tears, she continued, *"But even now, I know that whatever You ask of God, He will give You."*

With eyes that mirrored Martha's grief, Jesus said to her, *"Your brother will rise again"* (John 11:23).

Martha answered, *"I know that he will rise again in the resurrection on the last day."*

"I am the resurrection and the life. He who believes in

me will live, even though he dies; and whoever lives and believes in me will never die. Do you believe this" (John 11:25, 26 NIV)?

The air was oppressive, heavy and hot, almost unbearable. The sun beat down on their shoulders as they stood facing each other. A dog barked in the distance; a mother called out for her child; a fly buzzed around Martha's face. Time stood still for that instant before Martha replied, *"Yes, Lord, I believe that You are the Christ, the Son of God, who is to come into the world."*

In that quiet instant, Martha knew. She knew from the innermost part of her practical soul that Jesus was the Messiah. A seed of faith began to grow in her heart along with a joy that flushed over her, threatening to overwhelm her.

Jesus turned toward town and asked, "Where is Mary?"

"Lord, she just could not face you yet."

With a sad smile, Jesus said, "Bring Mary to me."

Martha hurried back to the house to find me. I was talking to a group of women who had come by to bring food and condolences. Excusing us, Martha took me off to the side and whispered, "The Teacher is here, and he is asking for you."

I looked at Martha. "What is it? What has happened to you?" Her sadness and despair had been replaced by a lightness of spirit. Could that be joy on her face?

Martha grabbed me and hugged me tight, telling me again, "The Teacher is asking for you."

I ran out the door. The women with me were so surprised and curious that they followed after me. I finally stopped running when I saw Jesus. His back was to me. I slowed my pace, allowing my heart and my emotions to calm down. He turned slowly toward me, sensing my approach. When I looked into his sorrowful eyes, I lost control. Falling to my knees, the cries welled up within my chest, strangling me with fresh grief. All the sorrow and disappointment of the last four days overcame me, and I cried out in anguish.

"Jesus, if you had been here, Lazarus would not have died. Where were you, Lord? Why did you not come? Why did you let us down?" I collapsed in a heap at his feet.

He knelt beside me and placed his hand on my shoulder. I sensed, rather than heard him pray. After a moment, he looked up at the people around us. *"Where have you laid him?"*

"Lord, come and see" (John 11:34 NIV).

Gently, he helped me up from the dusty road. As he did, I looked at him. Tears were running down his face. Unashamed, he wiped them away, and we began walking slowly toward Lazarus' tomb.

Along the way, I heard comments from the crowd of people that had gathered around us. I knew Jesus heard them, too.

"See how He loved him" (John 11:36 NIV).

"Well, why didn't he come and save him?"

"Could not he, who opened the blind eyes, keep his friend from dying?"

Jesus continued walking, but I knew by the way he quickened his pace and set his jaw that the comments upset him.

Martha caught up with us as we arrived at the tomb. By now the crowd had grown twice as big. The word had quickly spread that Jesus had finally arrived. The small-town grapevine had informed everyone about Martha sending word to Jesus, and how he did not come in time to save Lazarus. The people were curious as to what would happen next.

Without further delay, Jesus strode up to the cave where Lazarus was buried. He gestured to two of his disciples to remove the stone. Martha and I were horrified. She reached his side and grabbed Jesus' arm as if to restrain him. "Master, by this time there's a terrible smell. Lord, he's been dead for four days. What are you doing?"

Jesus looked down at Martha and said in a quiet but firm voice, *"Did I not tell you that if you believed, you would see the glory of God"* (John 11:40 NIV)?

Without waiting for an answer, Jesus turned back toward the disciples and said with a determined voice, "Go ahead, and take away the stone."

The crowd was dumbstruck. No one even moved. All eyes were on Jesus and the tomb as they slowly removed the stone.

Jesus raised his eyes to heaven and prayed, "Father, I'm grateful that you have listened to me. I know you always do listen, but because of the crowd standing here, I've spoken so that they might believe that you sent me."

With a loud shout, Jesus cried, *"Lazarus, come forth"* (John 11:43)!

As I held my breath, my heart began pumping out of control. I tried to focus on the opening of the tomb, but my eyes were brimming with tears. Martha grabbed my hand, squeezing so tight that it helped me focus.

We heard a sound from within the tomb, a shuffling noise like feet dragging through rocks. Suddenly, an apparition appeared in front of us. Could it be? My brain would not accept what my eyes were seeing. It was Lazarus. My precious brother, upright, trying to walk to us, encumbered by the shroud that was wrapped around him from head to toe. We couldn't even see his face, because it was still covered by the handkerchief. The crowd was stunned, fearful even, still not saying a word.

Jesus gestured toward Lazarus and asked his disciple to help him get out of his grave clothes. I could not allow myself to completely believe until they removed the handkerchief from Lazarus' face, and I saw him smile at me.

Lazarus was alive! My brother, who was dead, was truly alive. Martha and I, tears streaming down our faces, embraced Lazarus. Martha took his beloved face in her hands, crying, laughing, and praising God.

In the excitement of the moment, we lost sight of Jesus. By the time we returned to our home, he was gone.

The next few weeks were a blur as word about Lazarus spread throughout the neighboring villages. We heard that Jesus was forced to go to the village of Ephraim to remove himself from the crowds and the religious leaders. He was an enigma to all those in authority. Many people now believed in him because of the incredible miracle of raising Lazarus from the dead. This put him in further danger from the religious leaders, however.

Even Lazarus' life was in peril. Lazarus dismissed the danger to himself. What did he have to fear? He had met death and gone to the other side and back. He even said that it was difficult for him to leave the other side and come back to us because it was so glorious.

*****

It was almost time for the Passover. Martha and I were busy, as usual, getting ready for the guests that were sure to pass our door on their way to Jerusalem. We were in the kitchen when we heard Lazarus' voice. I turned toward the door and saw him enter, a huge smile on his face.

"Martha, Mary," he said. "We have guests."

Smoothing down our hair and dusting off our aprons, we waited as Lazarus stepped aside. It was Jesus. Like a little girl, I clapped my hands together and ran to hug him. Martha stood there and smiled, twisting her apron in her hand. She proclaimed, "We will have a feast in Your honor, Lord." He walked over to her and gave her his beautiful warm smile. "Thank you, Martha."

Martha and I were busy for the rest of the afternoon. This feast was going to be perfect in every way. We wanted Jesus to know how much we loved him and appreciated him. Lately, I had felt like my heart would burst with joy. It was more than the fact that Lazarus was now alive. Jesus showed all of us the meaning of the resurrection—he gave us a glorious glimpse into heaven. He allowed us to know the power of the Living God.

I wanted to do something to show him my appreciation. But what could that be? As I worked that afternoon, I came up with an idea. Martha and Lazarus might not understand, but I had to do this. I went to our hiding hole, the secret place where we kept our precious belongings. In here was a treasure chest filled with coins, silver, and gold. There were also beautiful and costly spices, perfumes, and oils that were reserved for the most sacred occasions. These spices and oils were probably more valuable than the gold and silver. We had already used up some of the expensive spices and oils when Lazarus had died. I reached in and brought out a bottle of pure nard, an exquisite perfume, and stuffed the precious offering deep down in the pocket of my skirt. Taking a deep breath, I prayed that God would bless my gesture. Now I must wait for the perfect time.

That evening, Martha served a feast. The food was delicious and filling, prepared to perfection. Martha blushed as the men complimented her on how delicious it was.

At the end of the meal, I knew the moment had come. Hesitantly, I approached Jesus. Our eyes locked as he smiled and nodded at me.

"Lord, may I?"

"Yes, Mary," he said quietly. "It is time."

I knelt at his feet and gently opened the flask of perfume. The sweet fragrance filled the room. I trickled the oil on his feet. As it dripped off his feet and onto the floor, I unbound my hair and began to wipe the excess perfume.

Everyone stopped talking and watched in fascination. Judas broke the silence by saying, *"Why was this fragrant oil not sold for three hundred denarii and given to the poor"* (John 12:5)?

Embarrassed, I gathered up my bottle of nard and started to rise, fearing that Jesus would scold me also. How could I have thought to do this to him? It seemed so right at the time, but now because of Judas, I felt foolish.

Jesus gently put his hand on my shoulder as I started to rise. Bowing my head in shame, I heard him say, *"Leave her alone, Judas. It was intended that she should save this perfume for the day of my burial. You will always have the poor among you, but you will not always have me"* (John 12:7, 8 NIV).

He helped me to my feet. As I stood, he looked me in the eye, and with a sad smile he said, "Thank you, Mary."

I did not see Him again after that. But the story did not end there, thank God. My Lord and Friend, Jesus Christ, was crucified one week later. But on the third day after he died, he rose from the dead. Before he ascended to heaven, he appeared to Lazarus. They spoke of the things to come because Lazarus understood.

We will devote the rest of our lives to Him. For you must understand . . . Jesus is our best friend.

The Transfiguration

Chapter Twenty

Matthew 16:13-17:13; Mark 9:1-13; Luke 9:18-36

"**J** ohn, wake up. It is time to leave."
I heard Peter call my name, but I couldn't seem to force myself to open my eyes. It was still dark outside, and the night had been so short. We had been up late the night before discussing all that had happened in the last two years. I pretended to ignore Peter for a few more minutes as I lay on my pallet and thought about our conversation last night. Had it been two years since I met Jesus? I had no idea on that fateful day two years ago where my life would lead. But how glad I am that I chose this path. What an incredible adventure. We never know what might happen each day. We have seen all kinds of miracles—people have been healed, four thousand were fed from seven loaves of bread and a few fish; we even saw Jesus raise a child from the dead.

We came to Caesarea Philippi six days ago. Jesus has explained a lot to us in this last week. He asked us one evening, *"Who do people say the Son of Man is"* (Matthew 16:13 NLT)? One of us replied, *"Some say John the Baptist, some Elijah, and others Jeremiah or one of the prophets."* Jesus then looked around at all of us and asked, *"But who do you say I am?"*

With only a moment's hesitation, Peter said, *"You are the Christ, the Son of the living God."* Jesus smiled at Peter and replied, *"You are blessed, for God, himself, has revealed this to you. I will build my church on you, Peter, for you are a rock. Hell will not prevail against you. Whatever you bind on earth will be bound in heaven, and whatever you loose on earth will be loosed in heaven."*

Jesus then looked intently at all of us and told us not to tell anyone that he was the Christ. The Christ . . . God's chosen one . . . the Messiah. My thoughts raced as I sat there in the room that night and listened to Jesus. I could not grasp the enormity of it. The Land of Israel has waited so long for a deliverer. We wondered among ourselves exactly how God was going to deliver us through Jesus.

Two nights later, we had gathered back together after supper. Jesus began to tell us things that we did not understand and did not want to hear. He told us that he must go to Jerusalem and suffer many things at the hands of the elders, chief priests, and teachers of the law. He also added that he must be killed.

Impetuously and with a fit of righteous anger, Peter grabbed Jesus and took him aside. *"Never, Lord!"* he said. *"This shall never happen to you"* (Matthew 16:22 NIV)!

With a firm voice, Jesus looked straight at Peter and said, *"Get behind me, Satan! You are a stumbling block to me; you do not have in mind the things of God, but the things of men"* (Matthew 16:23 NIV).

Peter was stunned; we all were. How could Jesus even speak that way to Peter? Then with a quiet and understanding voice, Jesus told Peter, "Come and sit down. You must listen to what I have to say. It may not be what you want to hear, Peter. But you must understand what is about to happen."

As they rejoined the group, Jesus explained that if we were to be his followers, we must take up our cross and follow him. He told us that there was to come a time when the Son of Man would come in His glory—accompanied by angels.

"*I tell you the truth,*" Jesus said looking at Peter, James, and me and said, "*some who are standing here will not taste death before they see the Son of Man coming in His kingdom*" (Matthew 16:28 NIV). We did not realize how soon we would understand what he meant. That was four days ago.

"John, you sleepyhead, get up or we will leave you behind!" This time it was Jesus who nudged me with his foot to get me awake. He was whistling to himself as we gathered up our belongings and left the house.

The early morning air was cool and still. We didn't say much as we began our hike. Finally, breaking the silence, I asked, "Where are we going, Lord?"

"We are going to meet some friends," he explained softly. He stopped and pointed ahead toward Mount Herman. "There is where our journey will end." The sun was beginning to come up behind the mountain, framing it with a glorious, golden fire. James and I looked at each other and shrugged. We settled our packs on our backs and continued walking.

The day was pleasant. Jesus always had a story to tell us. We laughed and talked quietly as we walked. Sometimes we would lapse into a comfortable silence —enjoying the scenery—the smells—the quiet sounds of nature.

We stopped at noon, halfway up the mountain, resting for a while, propped up against the shady side of a large boulder. The day had turned very warm, and we were grateful that we had brought along skins of water.

Jesus told us no more of the friends that we were to meet on the mountain. We had yet to see signs of anyone along our way.

Around five o'clock that evening, Jesus said, "We will stay here tonight." We camped along a bluff that overlooked the valley. It was a breathtaking view connecting the sky and the earth in one glorious landscape. I felt far removed from the crowds, the politics, and the grim reality of the valley.

We had brought along no food, as was Jesus' habit when he went alone to pray. So, we found our places along the bluff, each of us lost in our thoughts and prayers. Jesus was off away from us. I found myself watching him as he prayed. It was as if his entire body, soul, and spirit were in touch with his Father.

We watched the sun sink into the horizon, sending out waves of exquisite light and bathing the valley in hues of pink, brown, green, and blue. The evening settled over us. I'm afraid I was restless at times, having to get up from my place to stretch my legs. Jesus beckoned me to sit by him on the edge of the bluff. Sitting there beside him and talking gave me a sense of peace that calmed my restless spirit. We talked of home and our mothers and families. He told me a little about what to expect in times to come. I shared with him my worries and fears. Talking to Jesus was always so easy. He listened with his eyes as well as his ears. I never got the sense that he was bored or tired of my chatter.

After a while I joined James and Peter, leaving Jesus

to his prayers. We talked quietly late into the night, trying to stay awake. But the day had been long, and we found ourselves nodding off.

Something woke me—a cool wind maybe? I was disoriented for a minute, not even remembering where I was. James and Peter were awake also; I could hear them moving around close by. Did the same thing wake them?

I looked toward the bluff where Jesus had been praying. I could barely make out his silhouette in the dark. He was standing with his arms outstretched toward the heavens. Suddenly, an incredible thing happened. It started with his face. I could see him looking up toward the heavens. His face began to glow—a light that began softly and then got brighter. His eyes were closed at first, but then I could see him open them with a smile of acknowledgment. The light began to radiate from Jesus. His robe glistened as if it was made of brilliant white silk. It was not a reflection of light, but a light in and of itself. I had to put my hand above my eyes to protect them from the brilliant, intense light.

Peter, James, and I were all on our feet now, all traces of sleep gone. We were speechless; astounded at what we were seeing. Then to our complete surprise, we saw two men appear in front of Jesus. We were drawn closer as we heard him call their names, Moses and Elijah. How could this be? I looked at Peter and James; their faces showed the same incredible awe that I know I felt. My heart was pounding as I watched and listened.

They talked together like old friends, laughing at first, but their conversation then turning more serious. Moses and Elijah discussed Jesus' departure from Jerusalem as if it were a kind of exodus. Of course, we didn't comprehend at the time what this departure meant.

James, Peter, and I drew even closer to them. Always one to speak his mind, Peter said, *"Master, it is good for us to be here. Let us put up three shelters—one for you, one for Moses, and one for Elijah.* While Peter was speaking, we noticed a cool vapor-like cloud swirling at our feet. Brightening, it slowly rose and enveloped all of us. Blinded now by the brightness of the cloud, we heard a Voice, rich and deep, coming from the cloud. *"This is my Son, whom I love; with him I am well pleased. Listen to him"* (Matthew 17:5 NIV)!

Terrified, we fell to the ground. We lay there hiding our faces, trembling with fear. Jesus walked over and touched each one of us on the shoulder. When he came to me, he said, "John, get up, don't be afraid." Slowly I lifted my head, my eyes squinting in anticipation of the light. But the light was gone. Only Jesus stood there. Moses and Elijah had vanished, disappearing as they had appeared.

I rose to my knees, trying to stand. My legs were trembling so much that I decided instead to sit on the ground. James and Peter were sitting also. Jesus joined us.

We sat in silence for a while. I kept going over and over what had happened in my mind. Jesus allowed us this time to gather our thoughts. Had I dreamed this? Did Moses and Elijah appear here on the mountain? I looked at Jesus with new eyes, suddenly remembering what he had said to us earlier that week, *"I tell you the truth, some who are standing here will not taste death before they see the Son of Man coming in his kingdom."*

By this time, it was close to dawn. As soon as there was enough light, we began our trek down the mountain. On the way down, Jesus broke the silence by saying, "Don't tell anyone what you have seen here on this mountain."

I looked at Jesus in surprise, "Not tell, Lord? How do we keep something like this to ourselves?"

Then he said something I did not want to hear or accept. "John, you may talk about this after I have been raised from the dead."

Interlude Four

He Healed Them All

Luke 6:17-19

He healed them ALL
The multitude
Reaching out to him
Groping, Floundering, Fumbling
He healed them ALL
The tormented with unclean spirits
Helpless to fight off the
Demons within
He healed them ALL
The people who came to
Hear him, Worship him, Touch him
He healed them ALL
With power that
Went out of
Him
To heal the multitude.

Mary Magdalene

Chapter Twenty-One

*"And He Sent Away The Multitude, Got Into The Boat, And
Came To The Region Of Magdala" (Matthew 15:39).*

I felt the darkness. It was thick and black and . . . evil.
Where was it coming from? Was it real or in my
mind? Where was I? I must have wandered again. Looking
around, I realized that I had left the security of my miserable house. My home was beautiful and opulent but held
no happiness for me. The last I remembered, I was curled
up on my pallet, trying desperately to go to sleep.

Only in sleep can I survive. When I finally get to
sleep, it is like the sleep of the dead. Often, though, I find
myself awake in some strange place, not even remembering or knowing how I got there.

I groped around in the dark, listening fearfully.
Voices in my head drowned out all other sounds. Covering my ears, I sank to the ground screaming out in terror.

*****

I awoke again. It was daytime. I opened my eyes
to see light reflecting off the water. Squinting, I looked
around. I must have wandered down to the shores of the
Sea of Galilee. My muscles were aching, my mouth was

dry, and my heart was pounding. The voices in my head never shut up. I heard footsteps. Someone was walking toward me on the beach. Terrified, I curled up into a ball, silently crying out to God. Like an animal, I covered my head, making myself as small as possible, praying that the person would not notice me.

The footsteps stopped. The voices in my head were shouting, "Go away, go away!" Somehow, through the cacophony of noise, I heard someone call my name.

"Mary," the voice said softly. Then I heard it louder, "Mary."

The voices in my head shouted back, "Go away."

I dared to open my eyes, frantically looking around for a way to escape. My hair was falling in my eyes, and I had to brush it back to see. In front of me was a man. He was kneeling with his hand outstretched toward me.

Cowering, I cried out, "Please don't. Please don't touch me." I loathed men. All they had ever done was hurt and use me. The voices in my head kept repeating the mantra, "Go away, go away, go away, go away." I closed my eyes again, willing the voices to be quiet.

Minutes passed and the man did not come closer to me, nor did he leave. What did he want from me?

Once more I heard him call my name softly, "Mary." The voice was soothing, touching a part of me that I didn't even recognize. "Mary, look at me." Slowly I opened my eyes. "I am Jesus," he said simply. For reasons I did not understand, I was no longer afraid. It happened that quickly. At the mention of his name, I felt a warmth flow through me. The voices were still there, but his was stronger.

"Mary, you must listen very carefully to me," Jesus said. "I am going to command those spirits to come out of you. You must keep your eyes on me. Don't look away," he warned.

I could only nod mutely. As I looked into the man's eyes, he said, "Spirit, I command you to leave." He said this seven times. With each command, I felt an excruciating pain shoot through my head. It was difficult to focus my eyes on him, but I knew that I needed to do so.

Finally, after the seventh time, I was free, free of the spirits and free of the pain. Jesus walked over to me and took my hand to help me up. He said gently, "Mary, they are gone. They will not hurt you again." At his touch, I felt a warmth and energy flow through me like I had never felt before. A love that filled every part of my being, replacing all of the evil and pain. An unbelievable wave of happiness rose in my throat, and I laughed out loud with joy for the first time since I was a child. Jesus stepped back and crossed his arms, watching me, a huge smile on his face.

Like a child, I felt the urge to run, rejoicing in this happiness. I stretched out my arms, threw back my head, and ran toward the sea and down the beach. "I'm free! I'm free!" I shouted to the birds that flew above my head. Out of breath, I collapsed on the edge of the water, feeling the waves rippling gently around me. Another kind of wave hit me—a wave of emotion. This time, from the deepest part of my heart, I began to cry, great wracking sobs of pure happiness, cleansing every part of me.

Finally, exhausted and warmed by the glow that permeated my very soul, I looked up the beach to see Jesus sitting on a rock watching me and smiling. He was also looking out toward a boat that was coming our way.

He smiled at me. "Feeling better?" he asked.

"Who are you?"

"I am Jesus of Nazareth," he replied.

I had been so imprisoned and isolated by the emotions within me that I had no idea who this man was. Until now, my world had been the inside of my head.

He looked again toward the sea, this time waving. I followed his gaze toward a small fishing boat coming our way. Jesus stood up and cupped his hands around his mouth and shouted, "Peter, I am here!"

The man on the boat waved. "My friends are coming, Mary," he explained. "Do not be afraid. They have been out fishing this morning." He walked to the water's edge to help moor the boat. Unsure, I turned to walk back up the hill. As if sensing my hesitancy, Jesus said gently, "Mary, come. You must meet my friends."

"How was the fishing?" Jesus asked the men.

One man joked, "Master if you had been with us this morning, I know we would have done much better!"

Jesus laughed and said, "Sometimes, you must do this on your own, Peter."

Turning toward me, Jesus said, "Peter, James, and John, this is my new friend, Mary of Magdala." The men greeted me as if it were the most natural thing in the world to be introduced to a woman with wild hair and dirty clothes. Suddenly, I was very aware of my appearance. Sensing my discomfort, Jesus asked kindly, "Mary, will you join us?" He spoke to his friends, "We will take Mary to meet Joanna and Susanna. They are even now preparing the noonday meal at Salome's home." Explaining to me, he said, "Salome is the mother of these two fishermen, James and John. Their robust size is directly connected to their mother's cooking." He slapped the two on the back, threw back his head, and laughed.

I was taken in the boat to the other side of the Sea

of Galilee and handed over to a group of women who gathered me under their wings like mother hens. Salome continued her cooking while Joanna and Susanna drew up a bath of warm, sweet-scented water. Gently they washed and combed my tangled hair, let me soak in the heavenly water, and then afterward pulled over my head a beautiful gown of soft wool material.

During this administration of love, they began telling me their stories of Jesus, and the reason they had become one of his followers. Both Susanna and Joanna had come to Jesus at the same time but in two different ways. Susanna was soft-spoken and quiet. Joanna, wealthy and beautiful, was full of energy and as outspoken as a woman could be in those days. Her husband, Chuza, was Herod's steward. He had given up years ago trying to corral his beautiful, headstrong wife.

Susanna and Joanna had one thing in common; Jesus had healed them both. Susanna had been born with a crippled leg. Even though she had been blessed with a sweet and kind spirit, because of her affliction she had no hope of ever marrying. Joanna had contracted a terrible disease of the lungs which eventually wore a healthy body down to a shell.

In her soft, lilting voice, Susanna said, "I heard of this man, Jesus, who was traveling around Galilee teaching and healing the sick. I had to meet him."

Joanna chimed in, "Yes, rumors were flying all around Jerusalem. My husband would come home from Herod's court and tell me about him. I told Chuza that one day I would go and find this healer. I was desperate for a cure for my illness."

Smiling at Susanna, Joanna said softly, "We found him, didn't we Susanna?"

Nodding her head, Susanna turned toward me and explained. "Joanna and I met in Galilee. We, along with hundreds of others had come to hear Jesus and to be healed. We were sitting together along the side of a beautiful mountain. I remember that day like it was yesterday. It was warm and fragrant with the sweet smells of spring. Multi-colored wildflowers were scattered everywhere. The blue sky reached down and touched the mountains on the other side of the Sea of Galilee. I heard someone cough. The cough was ragged and harsh, causing me to turn toward the sound. Joanna was sitting there, pale and drawn, trying to catch her breath between coughs. Concerned, I offered her a drink of water from my pouch."

Joanna smiled at the memory and said, "I was so grateful to Susanna for offering to help me. I'm afraid my terrible cough discouraged anyone from sitting close to me, much less offering me help."

Luke 6:17-19

Joanna continued Susanna's story. "Soon, a hush fell over the crowd. Jesus had arrived. He was standing with his disciples on a level place beside the sea. We watched as people began to approach him. Amazed, we saw that people who touched him were healed of their affliction. Susanna and I patiently waited for our turn. Several hours passed as we slowly made our way down the mountain to Jesus. When we finally reached him, Susanna was ministered to first. I watched in absolute amazement as she stood there, balanced on her good leg and holding on to his hand for support. As he prayed for her, she gradually began to straighten her leg and let go of his hand, standing firmly on both feet. Tears were streaming down both of our faces by this time."

"Tirelessly, Jesus then turned to me. I will never forget the look in his eyes; for a moment my soul was lost in their depths. Instinctively, I reached out and touched the hem of his sleeve. A warmth began from the bottom of the soles of my feet, moved up my body, and radiated through my ragged lungs. I inhaled the sweet, life-giving air for the first time in two years. Impulsively, I reached out and hugged Jesus, not ever wanting to let him go."

"After a moment, he gently moved me away and said, 'Joanna, God has many great things for you to do. Your faith has saved you. Go in peace.'"

Suddenly Susanna jumped up and exclaimed, "Goodness, look at us sitting here talking. Joanna, we must finish lunch. Mary, we need your help. Will you join us?"

Luke 8:1-3

And so, my life began among the women who provided for Jesus and his followers. It was a sweet and blissful time, only to last for three short years. So many incredible events happened during this time. As for me, I felt loved for the first time in my life. The demons that plagued me were long gone, replaced by a sense of love that permeated my very soul.

We laughed. Jesus had the most incredible sense of humor. He would tell us stories about a God that I had never even imagined existed. We saw miracles that would have been impossible to believe if we had not experienced them or seen them with our very own eyes.

Joanna traveled between Galilee and Jerusalem to be with her husband and us. Susanna and I remained with Jesus and the others in Galilee. The other women who completed our group were Mary, Jesus' beautiful mother, the other Mary, who was the mother of James and Joses, Jesus' aunt, and of course, Salome. We were called "*the women who followed Him from Galilee.*" We were there, in the background, following closely behind the steps of Jesus. We were privileged to be his followers. We each had a special and unique relationship with the Master, growing closer to him every day. We served and provided for him, but we were never subservient to him.

✶✶✶✶✶

Three years passed quickly. It was the Passover once again, and we were with Jesus and his disciples in Jerusalem. We were looking forward to seeing Joanna again. One evening Susanna and I were cleaning up after a late Passover dinner when we heard a frantic knock on the door. It was Joanna's voice.

"Mary, let me in!" she cried.

I quickly went to the door to find Joanna standing there wringing her scarf in her hands and crying.

"Joanna, what is wrong?" I asked in concern.

She grabbed my hand and said in a frightened voice, "They have arrested Jesus. Chuza came home from Herod's court with the news."

"Dear God, no!" I cried. We had feared that this would happen.

"Where is he?" I asked

"My husband told me that they have taken Jesus to Pilate."

"Where are Peter and the others?"

Joanna shook her head, her expression full of pain. "Mary, they have all deserted him."

Joanna, Susanna, and I clung to each other for a moment and cried. Finally, breaking away from us, Joanna said in her typical, brisk way, "We will be there for him. We won't leave him to face this alone!"

I nodded. "We must find Mary and Salome to tell them. Jesus is Mary's son. She must know of this."

Susanna, Joanna, and I went to tell Mary the news of Jesus. Surprisingly, she heard the news with courage and strength. She hugged us and said, "We must go to him."

Joanna looked at all of us and said, "I will go and see if I can find out where he is now. Chuza will know." Placing her arm around Mary, she looked at all of us and said kindly, "You must stay here together until I get back."

It was a long night, the longest of our lives. Joanna did not come back until the early hours of the morning. When she finally did, her face told the story. She walked over to Mary and took her in her arms. "Mary," she said tearfully. Mary knew. She'd known for thirty-three years that this day would come.

Luke 23:49

We were there for him. We stood among the mocking crowd along the Via Dolorosa. We watched as he struggled through the streets, bleeding and torn, a crown of thorns on his head. How we wanted to go out there and lift that cross from his shoulders. We watched from a distance as they pounded the nails into his hands and feet, flinching with each blow of the hammer. We held our breath as we heard his screams of pain when they lifted him high into the air.

John joined us. Of all the men, John was the only one with the courage to be at Golgotha, the place where

Jesus was crucified. We all wanted to shield Mary from the pain. How could she stand there and watch her son suffer? As she had endured the pains of childbirth, she now had to endure the excruciating pain of his death.

I felt like I was back in the same suffocating cave of darkness that I had been in before Jesus had delivered me. The light of day began to grow dim.

"Oh, God!" I cried out, as I fell to my knees. "God, take away his pain. Don't forsake him. God help me."

The day had become as dark as night.

"Mary," a voice said. I felt the touch of a hand on my shoulder.

"Mary, it's over. He's gone."

It was John's voice I heard. He began gathering all of us together. I looked toward the cross. The sky was lightening now with the sun setting in the west, silhouetting the cross and Jesus' lifeless body.

John 19:38, 39

We saw two men talking and gesturing to a group of soldiers at the foot of the cross. John went to speak to them. He came back to us and explained, "One man's name is Joseph, and he has asked Pilate for Jesus' body. The other man is Nicodemus." John walked over to Jesus' mother and said, "Mary, Joseph wants to bury Jesus in his own tomb, and Nicodemus has brought a hundred pounds of myrrh and aloes."

Bewildered, Mary looked at John and then at the men standing and waiting at the foot of the cross. She nodded her head mutely, grateful for the strangers' kindness and generosity.

At her nod, Joseph asked the soldiers to help him take Jesus' body down from the cross. As they did so, we drew near. As they lowered his precious body to the ground, Mary knelt and cradled his head on her lap.

Joseph's servants gave us a beautiful linen shroud to wrap around his body. Lovingly, we did so. Joseph, Nicodemus, and John then carried Jesus and laid his body in the tomb. (Matthew 27:60).

"And the women who had come with Him from Galilee followed after, and they observed the tomb and how His body was laid. Then they returned and prepared spices and fragrant oils. And they rested, on the Sabbath according to the commandment" (Luke 23:55, 56).

We stood there for a long time, not speaking. It was dark and very quiet except for the sounds of the evening. We were numb with exhaustion. Surprisingly, it was Mary, Jesus' mother, who said softly, "There is nothing more to be done. We will gather the spices together and come back after the Sabbath is over."

Defeated and overcome by grief, we left the tomb and went to our homes. John took Mary and Salome home with him. Susanna and I went to Joanna's house to wait out another long night. None of us had slept for the last twenty-four hours. Joanna puttered about making pallets for each of us.

"We must rest," said Joanna in her brisk, no-nonsense way.

Weary, I curled up on the pallet, afraid to close my eyes, afraid of the horrifying pictures that awaited me in the dark. Thankfully, my exhaustion finally overcame my fear, and I slept.

We woke the next day, still in a state of shock and confusion. It was the Sabbath, so there was nothing we could do but sit and talk. Chuza had come home to tell us that rumors had been flying at Herod's court that the disciples were going to come and steal Jesus' body.

"I have heard that the chief priests and Pharisees gathered together to talk to Pilate. They reported to him that Jesus had told his disciples that after three days he would rise from the dead. They wanted Pilate to command that the tomb be made secure until the third day, lest his disciples come by night and steal him away and say to the people that he had risen from the dead," said Chuza.

"Steal his body?" Joanna asked bitterly. "The disciples are all in hiding. Do you think they are going to crawl out of their holes to steal his body?"

Chuza shook his head and continued. "Pilate believed them and gave them a guard to secure the tomb."

"Romans are guarding the tomb?" Joanna asked in disbelief. "What can Jesus do to them now? He is dead and his disciples are not going to bother him."

I understood her anger and bitterness. How could I ever forgive his disciples—his so-called friends—for deserting him?

Actually, unknown to Joanna and me at the time, the disciples had begun to reappear. Meekly and fearfully, they made their way back to the house where Mary, Salome, and John were staying. When Joanna, Susanna, and I went to the house later that day, they had all gathered— all, except Judas.

I don't know if I had ever seen or been around such a pathetic and defeated group of men. Peter, Andrew, James, and John were slouched in a corner, not talking, just standing and staring. Philip and Bartholomew were sitting on the floor, their backs to the wall, talking quietly with Matthew and James. Mary, of all people, was comforting Thomas, Thaddaeus, and Simon. We did not know what had happened to Judas.

Joanna, Susanna, and I did not stay long. We told Mary that we would gather our spices that evening after the Sabbath was over at sundown and meet the women at the tomb the next morning. She hugged us, and giving us her sweet smile, said "Thank you, my sisters. Your loyalty and love for my son will not be forgotten."

Joanna woke first the next morning, stumbling around in the dark, lighting the lamps for us. We did not talk as we dressed, each of us lost in our own thoughts. We gathered up the precious vials of spices and ointments in our aprons and left the house. A short time later, we met up with Mary, the mother of James, and Salome.

Making our way in the darkness, only Joanna spoke as we walked, voicing a question that we all had. *"Who will roll away the stone when we get to the tomb?"* (Mark 16:3).

Salome answered bitterly, "Perhaps we can wake the soldiers who guard the tomb. Surely, they are not afraid of a group of women."

As we drew near the place where Jesus lay entombed, we sensed that something was wrong. It was still dark, making it difficult to see, but as we came closer with our torches, we found to our amazement and shock that the stone had been rolled away.

I gasped in dismay, "Lord God, what has happened?"

Terrified, we walked slowly toward the tomb. Looking to our left, we saw that the soldiers were lying sprawled out on the ground, their weapons scattered beside them. We thought they were dead.

I reached the opening of the tomb first with Joanna

close behind me. Strangely, we noticed a faint light coming from within the tomb. Hesitantly, we stooped and walked inside.

Mark 16:5-7

Startled, I saw a young man clothed in a long white robe, sitting on the right side of the cave. "Oh." I cried out.

"*Do not be alarmed,*" he said. "*You seek Jesus of Nazareth, who was crucified. He has risen! He is not here. See the place where they laid Him.*"

"*But go, tell His disciples*—and Peter——*that He is going before you into Galilee; there you will see Him, as He said to you.*"

Amazed, I looked at the young man and then at the linen shroud lying like a deflated cocoon on the stone ledge. Dumbly, I whispered to myself, "Is this true?" Did I dare believe that Jesus had risen from the dead? I saw him die. I watched the soldiers thrust a sword into his side. I helped wrap this very shroud around his lifeless body. I looked around at the women, each one standing there in shock.

In a ragged voice, Joanna said, "*We must go find Peter.*" (Luke 24:10)

Dropping our bundles of spices and ointments, we backed out of the tomb. Picking up our skirts, we began to run, not stopping until we came to the house where Peter and John were staying.

I pounded on the door. "Peter, John, open the door."

Finally, Peter peeked out, frightened at first, not knowing for sure who was pounding. We all began speaking at once. Not understanding a word, Peter finally grabbed me and said, "Mary, what are you saying to me?"

Tears streaming down my face, I said, "Peter, Jesus is alive."

Luke 24:11

Angrily, Peter shook me and asked, "What nonsense is this you speak? What kind of idle tales do you spread, Woman?"

Unperturbed, I answered patiently, "Peter, John, come and see for yourself. He is no longer in the tomb. An angel told us that Jesus has risen from the dead."

Peter studied our faces carefully. Seeing the joy, he turned around to look at John. John's face was wreathed in a huge smile. Peter just shook his head.

John said, "Peter, we must go to the tomb."

John took off running. Peter hesitated for a moment. I looked at him, reading the pain and guilt on his face.

"Peter, you must do this. You must go and see."

John 20:3-18

Daring to hope, Peter followed John to the tomb, and I trailed close behind. When Peter and I arrived at the tomb, John ran up to us.

"I looked in and saw the linen cloths, just as you said, Mary." Grabbing Peter's sleeve, he said, "Come and see, Peter."

Still not believing, Peter entered the tomb. He walked slowly over to the shroud lying empty on the stone shelf. He gently touched the handkerchief that had been around Jesus' head. It was folded neatly together in a place by itself.

John walked up beside him and said, "Peter, Jesus is

alive."

Peter shook his head, not daring to believe. "It cannot be, John. This cannot be true."

Finally, John squeezed Peter's shoulder and said, "We must go and tell the others what we have seen."

They left me standing at the tomb. I walked slowly over to a nearby rock and sat down to think. I looked around, noticing for the first time that the soldiers had gone. They must have left in a hurry because their spears were still lying scattered on the ground. The men's voices began to fade into the distance. It was so quiet. I felt the warmth of the morning sun as it peeked its way through the trees in the garden.

Doubts began to form in my head again. Overwhelmed by all of the possibilities, I put my hands over my face and began to cry. All of my hopes and dreams had died with Jesus. I loved Him. How can I explain this love? It was not the same love that a wife has for a husband or a mother has for her child. This love was created in my spirit that morning three years ago along the shore of the Sea of Galilee.

And now, coming here and finding the empty tomb, the grave cloths, and the angel—did I dare allow myself to believe? Where was He? Was this some cruel joke?

"Woman, why are you crying?"

Startled, I turned around to see a man standing beside a beautiful, gnarled olive tree. The morning sun was behind him, shining in my eyes, so I couldn't get a very good look at his face. I squinted through blurry, swollen eyes trying to see who the man was.

I thought he was the gardener. Perhaps he knew what had happened to Jesus. As if reading my mind, he spoke again. "Are you looking for someone?"

I nodded numbly and pointed toward the tomb. "My Master, Jesus of Nazareth, was buried in this tomb three days ago. The tomb belongs to Joseph of Arimathea, but he permitted us to use it. And now Jesus' body has vanished."

I knew I was rambling and not making very much sense. I squinted toward the man and said, *"Sir, if You have carried Him away, tell me where You have laid Him, and I will take Him away"* (John 20:15).

Wondering to myself how I was going to accomplish such a feat, I turned back toward the empty tomb.

"Mary."

The instant I heard him say my name, I knew—I knew that voice. It was the same quiet voice that called my name along the shore of the Sea of Galilee.

Trembling, I slowly turned around. He was standing directly in front of me, smiling that wonderful smile.

"Teacher!"

I could not stand. I fell to my knees at his feet and worshiped Him. Gently, Jesus reached down and helped me to my feet.

"Do not cling to Me, for I have not yet ascended to My Father" (John 20:17).

"Listen carefully to what I have to say to you. *Don't be afraid! Go tell my brothers to leave for Galilee, and they will see me there"* (Matthew 28:10 NLT).

I didn't want to leave Him again—to let Him out of my sight. I wanted to hold on to Him and never let go.

"Go now, Mary," he urged gently. "I will never leave you or forsake you again. I will be with you always."

Reluctantly, I left Him. When I turned and looked one more time, he was gone. All of a sudden, the realization of what truly happened bubbled up inside of me, and I ran to share my good news.

Jesus Christ is alive. I saw Him—talked to Him. Of all people, He chose me to be the one to have the privilege of sharing the Good News.

When I burst into the house with my news, Mary was there. She was sitting in a chair by the door, her hands folded serenely on her lap, waiting. I walked over to her and knelt beside her. Taking her hands in mine, I said, "Mary, I saw Him." Tears of joy began running down her cheeks.

"He is alive?" she whispered. I smiled and nodded at her.

I looked around at all the stunned faces of those gathered around us. Still holding Mary's hand, I stood up and declared, "He spoke to me. He said to tell you that *He was ascending to His Father and your Father, His God and your God.* But He wants to see you first."

Luke 24:13-35

That evening we were all gathered together when Mary's husband, Cleopas, came in with the most wonderful story. He and another man were walking toward the town of Emmaus, discussing all that they had heard that day.

"As we were walking, we noticed a man coming up behind us on the road," said Cleopas. "He asked us what we were talking about that was making us so sad."

Cleopas stopped speaking, still not believing what had happened. Mary, his wife, begged him to continue.

Taking a deep breath, he continued. "I asked him if he was the only stranger in Jerusalem who did not know what had happened."

"'What has happened?' he asked us."

"I told him Jesus' story of how he was crucified and then was said to have risen from the dead."

Cleopas stopped once again and looked around at all of us.

I found I was holding my breath. "Cleopas," I said, gently.

He shook his head and once again continued.

"The man said to us, '*O foolish ones, and slow of heart to believe in all that the prophets have spoken.' Ought not the Christ to have suffered these things and to enter into His glory?*'"

"By this time, we had arrived at Emmaus. It was suppertime and we were both hungry and exhausted from the day. The stranger bid us good-bye and continued walking down the road. I felt suddenly impelled to call out to him. I asked him to remain with us since the night was drawing near. I could not let him leave. At first, he seemed reluctant, but we both urged him to stay the night with us at Emmaus."

Cleopas stopped his story once again as if to catch his breath. I walked over to him and placed my hand on his shoulder. Of all people, I knew why this story was so difficult to tell—so unbelievable. I smiled and encouraged him to continue.

"We had not eaten the whole day, so we quickly gathered together a meal of wine, fish, bread, and cheese. After we sat down, I asked the stranger if he would bless our food. He nodded his head and took the bread in his hands, blessed and broke it, and gave it to us. As he handed the bread to me, our eyes met, and I saw him for the first time."

Cleopas looked around at our stunned faces. "It

was Him. It was Jesus—He is alive."

Peter walked over to Cleopas, his eyes burning intently, and asked, "What did he say? Where did he go?" Cleopas shrugged his shoulders and said honestly, "He just vanished, Peter. One moment he was there in front of me, and then he was gone."

"One thing I do know, our hearts burned within us while He talked with us on that road, and while He opened scriptures to us."

There was silence in the room when Cleopas finished his story. I sat down beside his wife, Mary. Her face showed the exhaustion that I felt. I sat there on the floor, closed my eyes, and laid my head back against the wall, trying to still my weary mind.

Luke 24:36-49

Suddenly, Jesus, Himself, was standing in the room with us.

"Peace to you." His voice was clear and strong.

Some of the disciples were fearful, backing away from Him as if He were a ghost. I was unafraid. I smiled up at Him, my physical and mental exhaustion gone. I rose to my feet, my eyes fixed on Him. He looked at me and smiled, His smile acknowledging my faith in His resurrection.

"Why are you frightened?" he asked. *"Why do you doubt who I am? Look at my hands. Look at my feet. You can see that it's me. Touch me and make sure that I am not a ghost, because ghosts don't have bodies, as you see that I do"* (Luke 24:38, 39 NLT). His smile lit the room.

The disciples stood still, looking at Jesus and then each other. Their faces showed a mixture of shock and joy. Understanding their doubt, Jesus turned toward me, and with humor in His voice, said, "Mary do you have anything to eat?" Knowing how much Jesus loved food, I laughed and went to find Him a piece of broiled fish. He sat down at the table, and the disciples edged closer to Him. As we watched in awe, He hungrily ate the fish, and then followed the small meal with a couple of swallows of red wine.

Finally, He pushed back from the table and gestured for the disciples to gather around Him. Starting with Matthew, He reached out and clasped each disciple's hand, saying, *"This is what I told you while I was still with you, that all things must be fulfilled which were written in the Law of Moses and the Prophets and the Psalms concerning Me. And now you are witnesses to these events. Wait in Jerusalem until you are filled with power from on high. As the Father has sent Me, I also send you"* (John 20:21).

And with that, He breathed on them and said, *"Receive the Holy Spirit"* (John 20:22).

And then He was gone.

*****

I, Mary Magdalene, am also a witness to the resurrection of my Lord, Jesus Christ. I received the powerful infilling of the Holy Spirit. I was there at Pentecost when the Holy Spirit filled all of us with joy and His love. I, too, shared the Good News of Jesus Christ and His forgiveness. Susanna and I were blessed to stay with Jesus' mother until she went to be with the Lord several years later. We were privileged to share the Good News with everyone that Jesus Christ is alive, and His love, forgiveness, and healing are available to every man, woman, and child on earth. Amen

John

Chapter Twenty-Two

Luke 22

I t was the Passover. Two times already I had shared the sacred meal with Jesus and the apostles. This year would make the third. This time, somehow, everything seemed different. Peter and I were discussing just that as we made our way through the busy streets of Jerusalem. We were to meet Jesus at the temple. It had been his habit lately to spend the night on the Mount of Olives and then meet us at the temple in the morning to speak to the people.

Yes, Peter agreed that Jesus had been different lately. It had become very dangerous for him in Jerusalem, but that did not seem to upset him. He spent even more time in prayer and then told us all kinds of strange things that left us feeling confused and disquieted.

When we met Jesus at the temple that morning, he gave instructions to Peter and me. *"Go and make preparations for us to eat the Passover"* (Luke 22:8 NIV).

Always the practical one, I asked, *"Lord, where do you want us to prepare for it"* (Luke 22:9 NIV)?

Smiling, he said, *"Go into the city. A man carrying a jug of water will meet you there."* He then gave us further instructions as to how we were to prepare this special Passover meal.

Peter and I left immediately, not doubting at all that a man would be there to meet us. Peter saw him first as we weaved through the crowd of people. Peter called out to the man. Waving, the man pushed through the crowd and made his way over to us. He asked us to follow him and led us down a long, winding street, stopping in front of his house.

We explained that the Teacher would like for him to show us the guest room where we would eat the Passover meal. He nodded and asked us to follow him again. We walked up the stairs to a large upper room. It was furnished with a round table and comfortable cushions on the floor. I guess because we looked surprised, he explained how Jesus had already arranged all of this. He said he was at the temple one morning listening to Jesus. He was surprised when afterward Jesus asked to speak to him alone. Jesus explained that he would like to find a place to celebrate the Passover that would not be known to the crowds. The man told Jesus that he was honored that Jesus trusted him, and he offered his home to Jesus and his friends.

Peter and I began to make preparations. The man offered his kitchen and his wife to help cook the Passover meal. We were grateful for the help.

Late that afternoon we found Jesus praying again on the Mount of Olives. Walking toward him, we heard the shofar sound from the temple as they sacrificed the Passover lamb. Jesus raised his head and slowly stood, looking off toward Jerusalem. Were those tears in his eyes? Peter and I both felt an unexplainable sense of loss.

Trying to shake off the melancholy, Peter told

Jesus that we had accomplished our task. I explained that we had told the others where and when we were celebrating the Passover meal that evening.

We gathered together, all thirteen of us, around the table that night. How many years had we all celebrated the Passover? It was a very special time for the Jewish people. Something was amiss this night, however. We could all sense it. Later we realized it was a Passover meal that would change the course of time and history.

I sat at Jesus' right side, a place of honor. Sometimes I saw myself as Jesus' younger brother. There was a kinship between us that was very special. Peter, James, and I were with Jesus when he healed Jairus' little daughter. We were also with him on the mountain when Moses and Elijah appeared. He must have trusted us to allow us to experience those events with him.

Jesus looked at all of us and said, *"I have eagerly desired to eat this Passover with you before I suffer. For I tell you, I will not eat it again until it finds fulfillment in the kingdom of God"* (Luke 22:15, 16 NIV).

He picked up the Passover cup and said, *"Take this and divide it among you. For I tell you I will not drink again of the fruit of the vine until the kingdom of God comes"* (Luke 22:17, 18 NIV).

It was very warm in the room. We passed the cup, drinking the sweet wine and thinking of how the angel of death had "passed over" the children of Israel.

Then Jesus said something very confusing to us at the time. It was not in keeping with the traditional Passover celebration. He took the bread, gave thanks and broke it, and gave it to each of us. He said, *"This is my body given for you; do this in remembrance of me"* (Luke 22:19 NIV).

After supper, we continued to sit around the table quietly talking together. Suddenly, Jesus took the Passover cup, and he held it up. We all looked toward Him wondering what he was going to say next. *"This cup is the new covenant in my blood, which is poured out for you"* (Luke 22:20 NIV). He asked us to drink from the cup. With questioning eyes, we did so. He then looked around the table and said calmly, *"But the hand of him who is going to betray me is with mine on the table. The Son of Man will go as it has been decreed, but woe to that man who betrays him"* (Luke 22:21, 22 NIV).

We were all dismayed at what he had just said and began talking nervously with each other. Peter gestured to me across the table. "What did he say?" he mouthed. I shook my head and frowned. I noticed that Jesus turned and said something to Judas. He left soon after. I assumed it was to run an errand for Jesus.

Our conversation then turned toward one of our favorite subjects. Many of us felt like Jesus was going to bring in a new kingdom—one that would overthrow the Roman rule and bring peace to our country. We often dreamed of our place in that kingdom and wondered who would be the greatest and rule at Jesus' side. How could we have been so wrong that night?

Jesus listened to us ramble on and then put a stop to the direction that our conversation was going. He told us that there would be a place for us in his kingdom, but his kingdom was different from any that we could imagine. His kingdom was one of service where *"he who is greatest among you, let him be as the younger, and he governs as he who serves."*

Jesus then looked directly at Peter, calling him by his given name. *"Simon, Simon, Satan has asked to sift you as wheat. But I have prayed for you, Simon, that your faith may not fail. And when you have turned back, strengthen your brothers"* (Luke 22:31, 32 NIV).

Peter replied, *"Lord, I am ready to go with you to prison and to death"* (Luke 22:33 NIV).

Jesus sadly answered him, *"I tell you, Peter, before the rooster crows today, you will deny three times that you know me"* (Luke 22:34 NIV).

We were stunned when we heard Jesus say this. Peter was so strong and sure of himself. He was loyal to a fault. How could it be that he would deny Jesus?

Jesus reached out with a reassuring hand and touched Peter's shoulder. Then changing the subject, he reminded us of the time he sent us out to preach in the countryside without a purse, bag, or even sandals. Now, he said, we must be prepared to pay our own way. There would be dangerous times ahead, and we would need defense and protection. "You are associated with me," he explained, "and I will be numbered with the transgressors as a criminal."

In answer to that, we showed Jesus two swords that we had there with us in the room. He shrugged, dismissed the idea, and said, *"It is enough"* (Luke 22:38).

We left the upper room soon after that. We were a rather somber and quiet group as we walked with Jesus to the Mount of Olives. When we reached the Garden of Gethsemane, Jesus asked all of us to pray with him.

He told the others to stay at the foot of the mountain and then took Peter, James, and me along with him up the path. A short distance later, He stopped suddenly and said, *"My soul is overwhelmed with sorrow to the point of death. Stay here and keep watch"* (Mark 14:33, 34 NIV).

Peter, James, and I sat down on the ground and

tried to pray. We didn't understand what was happening. We knew Jesus was troubled, but we didn't know how to help him. Looking back, we later realized that the only support Jesus had that night was from God. As we each walked our own road of sorrow, we remembered and knew that God was the one and only Person that we could truly depend upon.

Jesus said, *"Pray that you will not fall into temptation"* (Luke 22:40 NIV). Then he walked about a stone's throw away from us. The night was cool, almost cold, but fragrant with the smells of early spring. I saw Jesus kneel down; he prayed quietly for a while. Then in an audible voice that carried across the garden, I heard Jesus say, *"Abba, Father, all things are possible for You. Take this cup away from Me; nevertheless, not what I will, but what You will"* (Mark 14:36).

What could this mean? I heard the sorrow in his voice. It cut into my heart like a knife. I also felt fear like I had never felt before. At that moment, I looked toward Jesus and blinked my eyes. An angel was standing beside him. They spoke quietly with each other. The light of the angel shone on Jesus as he prayed, and it was then that I saw his face. His anguish was so great that he had begun to sweat drops of blood. Looking at him, I experienced sorrow that I had never before felt and never would feel again in my life.

The angel went away, and Jesus continued to pray quietly. I was exhausted, emotionally and physically. The next thing I knew, Jesus was shaking Peter gently on the shoulder. *"Why are you sleeping?"* he asked. *"Get up and pray so that you will not fall into temptation"* (Luke 22:46 NIV). This was the second time that Jesus told us to pray so that we would not fall into temptation....what does this even mean?

Peter

Chapter Twenty-Three

Luke 22:47-62

I sat up groggily, trying to focus on what Jesus was saying to me. I looked up to see him turn toward the sound of a mob coming up the path through the garden. A crowd of men carrying torches approached us. The crowd included the leading priests, the captains of the temple guard, and the elders, all led by our very own brother, Judas Iscariot. His face was set and void of expression. Why was he here leading this group? Judas approached Jesus to greet him. Even in the mayhem, I heard Jesus say, *"Judas, are you betraying the Son of Man with a kiss"* (NIV)?

I was overcome by rage. Grabbing a tight hold on my sword, I heard someone say, "Lord, shall we strike with the swords?" And without even thinking, I swung mine, striking the servant of the high priest and cutting off his ear.

Jesus immediately reached out and grabbed my arm, "No, Peter, I will not permit this!" He knelt beside the fallen servant and placed his hand on the servant's ear. For an incredible moment, everyone stopped and watched while Jesus replaced and healed the ear.

Jesus stood up, looking directly at the priests, elders, and the captains of the temple. With a resigned and composed voice, he said, *"Am I leading a rebellion, that you have come with swords and clubs? Every day I was with you in the temple courts, and you did not lay a hand on me. But this is your hour—when darkness reigns."*

Their faces were set like stone, angry and defiant. The captain of the guard arrested Jesus and bound his hands behind his back. He roughly pushed him toward the path down the mountain to Jerusalem.

John and I followed at a distance, but the other men fled into the night. How could this be happening? We stumbled along the dark path, wondering where they were taking Jesus. Fear rose in my throat, and I had to stop along the path to vomit the bitter bile that was threatening to strangle me.

They took him to the home of Annas, the father-in-law of Caiaphas. John was acquainted with the high priest, so he was allowed to enter the courtyard. I stayed behind, outside the gates in the street. It was cold outside, and the fire inside the courtyard looked inviting, but fear held me back. After a time, John came to the gate with the servant girl who was on duty there, and she let me in. As I sat down close to the light of the warm fire, the girl frowned at me and asked, "Aren't you one of Jesus' disciples?"

Staring at the fire, I replied, *"I am not"* (John 18:17 NIV)!

Later, another man around the fire spoke up, "I know I've seen you with Jesus." I looked up at him and said firmly, "I told you, I don't know him!"

In the meantime, John eased his way toward the door of Annas' house. He heard the high priest questioning Jesus. *"I have spoken openly to the world,"* Jesus replied. *"I always taught in synagogues or at the temple, where all the Jews come together. I said nothing in secret. Why question me? Ask those who heard me. Surely, they know what I said"* (John 18:20, 21 NIV).

When Jesus said this, one of the officials nearby struck him in the face. *"Is this the way you answer the high priest"* (John 18:22 NIV)?

Jesus stood up a little straighter and replied with a firm voice, *"If I said something wrong, tell me why it is wrong. If I told the truth, why did you strike me?"*

Annas had nothing to say to that, so he dismissed him and sent Jesus, still bound, to Caiaphas, the high priest.

While Annas was interrogating Jesus, I stayed out in the courtyard, continuing to warm my hands at the fire and wait. My mind was numb. A man walked up to the fire and stared at me as the servant girl did. Pointedly he said, "Didn't I see you in the garden with Jesus?" Looking around and addressing the group standing near the fire, he said with disdain, "This man is obviously a Galilean."

Angrily, I spoke in a voice louder than I intended, "Man, I don't know what you are talking about." At that moment, I looked up to see them bringing Jesus out of the door of Annas' house into the courtyard. He looked straight at me with a look of sadness that will go with me for the rest of my life. In the distance a rooster began to crow, reminding me of what Jesus had said earlier that evening at the Passover meal. *"Peter, when you hear the rooster crow today, you will have denied me three times."*

What had I done? What kind of coward was I? I watched as they led Jesus out of the courtyard and out of my sight. They were taking away my best friend, my Master. Why hadn't I stopped them? Oh, God! How could this be happening?

I stumbled out of the courtyard and into the filthy street. Finding a dark, dirty corner on the street, I fell to my knees and wept bitterly.

Simon of Cyrene

Chapter Twenty-Four

Mark 15:21

*A passerby named Simon, who was from Cyrene,
was coming in from the countryside just then, and
the soldiers forced him to carry Jesus' cross. (Simon
was the father of Alexander and Rufus.)*

It was the festival of the Passover. I had traveled a great distance to be here. There was always a yearning in my spirit to be in Jerusalem to celebrate this wondrous event. It was so crowded in the city that I was forced to seek shelter outside of Jerusalem.

Jerusalem! The City of David. How I had longed to be here.

I woke early that Friday morning just to be able to walk the quiet streets, to see the temple, to worship God. The quiet that I yearned for was not to be, however.

I heard the commotion before I saw it. People were crowded along the street as if to watch a parade. I pushed my way through the throng. "What is going on?" I asked a man standing quietly among the crowd. "It is a crucifixion," he replied. There was something in his voice that made me turn and look at him. His face was pale with grief.

"Who are they crucifying?" I asked. "Do you know him?"

"Yes, he is my Master and my friend," the man said in a hoarse whisper. The man stepped behind me and was swallowed by the crowd.

Even more curious, I found myself on the edge of the street. I saw a legion of Roman soldiers coming toward me. They were paying especially close attention to one of the three men carrying their crosses. This man was stumbling under the load—falling to the ground and then struggling to get back on his feet. There was something about the man that caught my attention. What was that on his head? A crown of thorns? He was being mocked and ridiculed as he struggled down the street, trying to carry the heavy load on his back. I sensed a dignity about the man and found myself mesmerized, unable to take my eyes off of him.

In my daze, I failed to notice the Roman soldier coming toward me. As I watched the man fall one more time under his heavy load, the soldier grabbed my arm, and I felt the cold steel of a blade at my neck.

"You," he demanded. "You help him carry the cross."

I had no choice but to follow the soldier. The man was on his knees, his head down, his back streaked with blood. Silently, I lifted the heavy beam off of his back. He looked at me gratefully and slowly stood up, weaving unsteadily, obviously in great pain.

A group of women followed us, mourning and wailing. He turned toward them and told them not to cry for him, but for Jerusalem, themselves, and their children.

We walked to the place called Golgotha, or "The

Skull." The other two men were led with us, one cursing and crying out, the other one quiet. Arriving at the scene, I slowly laid the crossbar onto the ground at the man's feet.

Reluctantly I turned to go, but something held me back. Was it his eyes or the kingly way he stood there, just waiting? He seemed so alone. What could this man have done to warrant this? Intuitively, I knew that he deserved none of it.

I decided to stay. Why I do not know, but I needed to be there. I watched, horrified, as they nailed Him to a cross and lifted him high in the air. On both sides of him hung two common criminals; one was screaming out in anger, the other in pain.

Luke 23:34-43

I heard him say the strangest thing. *"Father, forgive them, for they do not know what they do."* Why did I feel a sense of guilt when I heard this?

The soldiers, bored with their duties, began casting lots for his clothes. People were standing close to me, obviously religious rulers, sneering and saying, *"He saved others; let Him save Himself if He is the Christ, the chosen of God."*

What was this all about? I turned toward a man standing with a group of women. "Who is this man?" I asked. "What has he done that they would crucify him?"

He looked at me, tears streaming down his face. "His name is Jesus. He has done nothing wrong." He began to tell me about Jesus, the miracles that he performed, the people that he touched. My eyes were fixed upon the crucified man as I heard his incredible story.

The time passed. By now we were all exhausted by

the pain and anguish that Jesus was suffering. I heard one of the criminals that hung beside Jesus curse and scream out, *"If You are the Christ, save Yourself and us."* The other criminal rebuked him and said, "We are criminals and deserve to be punished. This man has done nothing wrong." He then looked at Jesus and said, *"Lord, remember me when You come into Your kingdom."*

Jesus answered him, *"Assuredly, I say to you, today you will be with me in Paradise."*

A strange thing began to happen around noon. The sky started to gradually turn dark as if an evil force were swallowing up the sun. Darkness fell over the city; we even heard roosters start to crow.

Everyone was quiet. Even the soldiers had ceased their play. The religious leaders, feeling nervous and uncomfortable, slipped away to the temple. Few people remained in the darkness.

I eased closer to the cross with the small group of women and the one remaining man. I heard Jesus speak to the man. He asked him to take care of his mother.

At about three o'clock, Jesus cried out in a loud voice, *"Eloi, Eloi, lama sabachthani?"* (Mark 15:34). The desolation and fear that I felt in and around me seemed to engulf me. I fell prostrate to the ground and covered my head, crying into the rocks and dirt. God had truly deserted that hill. Only fear and suffering remained.

Someone ran to get Jesus a sponge soaked with wine vinegar. Refusing the drink, he cried out again—this time incredibly with a voice of triumph. Slowly I rose to my feet. I looked up to the cross and saw his head slump forward. I saw him die.

At that moment, a rumbling came from the inmost part of the earth. The ground began to shake beneath my feet, and the rocks vibrated and bounced around me. For some reason, this did not frighten me. I fell to my knees, raised my hands to the sky, and shouted out to God. The Spirit of God had returned to that place.

Gradually the sky began to lighten. The women who were watching were led away by the man I had talked to earlier, the man who told me all about Jesus. His name was John.

I had so many questions. Was it over? Who was this man, who claimed to be the Son of God? Why did they crucify an innocent man? I had carried his cross; was I also responsible for his death? I slowly made my way back through Jerusalem. The city was strangely quiet. As I walked by the temple, I heard two priests talking excitedly about what had happened that afternoon. It seems the temple curtain, the very one separating the Holy of Holies from the rest of the temple, had been torn in two from the top to the bottom. (Mark 15:38).

I spent that night outside of the gates of the city. The next morning was the Sabbath. I could not face going to the temple and seeing those same priests and Pharisees, the very ones who had crucified Jesus. The ugly looks of hatred on their faces that terrible day will stay with me forever.

I observed that Sabbath day alone with my thoughts—a stranger to this country and now to this religion, a religion that puts a man to death—a man who has done no wrong.

Thank God, my story does not end here. I stayed in Jerusalem for several more weeks because something incredible happened. A rumor began to circulate that Jesus was no longer dead. A group of women, some of whom had stood with us on that terrible hill, had gone to the tomb to find it empty. An angel was sitting there and told them that Jesus was alive.

I did not know what to make of this story. How could this be? I carried his cross; I saw him die . . . I had to find out more. I had to find John. After standing there with him at the crucifixion, I knew that he would now trust me. It took me several days to locate him. After making inquiries of people on the street, I finally found the house where he was staying.

"Is it true? Is he really alive?" John had no more shut the door when these questions spilled out of me. Before he answered, I knew. His face was alight with joy.

"Yes, Simon," he said. "Jesus is alive!"

I had so many questions; I didn't know where to begin. We must have talked for hours. As I was getting ready to leave, John said, "Simon, go with us to Galilee. He said that he would meet us there." I looked at John and smiled. "Oh, yes. I will go with you."

It was in Galilee that I met my risen Lord. A group of us had gathered along the shores of the Sea of Galilee. I remember it being a beautiful, clear morning. The waves were lapping softly against the sandy shore and the mountains loomed behind us, crisp and green against the morning sky. The disciples were there helping Peter and John mend their fishing nets, reminiscing about Jesus and laughing and talking about all of the wonderful things that Jesus had said and done. All of a sudden, there he was in the midst of us. Yes, it was true. Jesus was alive. I saw him for myself. He looked directly at me with a smile of thanks, so different from the look of agony that I had seen on his face when I lifted the cross from his back.

He began to share many things with us. With all of this in mind, I knew that I must stay in Palestine for a while longer before I returned to my home in Cyrene. Jesus told us to linger in Jerusalem, because the Holy Spirit would come upon us, giving us power from on high.

I followed the disciples back to Jerusalem, falling into a routine of worshipping each morning in the temple, spending the afternoons reminiscing, and praying together in the evenings. We were just . . . waiting.

Acts: 1, 2

One evening, Peter stood up and said it was necessary to choose a man to replace Judas. Two men's names were proposed, Justus and Matthias. The disciples prayed and cast lots. The lot fell to Matthias, so he was added to the eleven apostles.

The day of Pentecost finally came. It had now been fifty days since Jesus rose from the dead. We were all gathered together praying and worshipping God. There were about a hundred and twenty of us, all of the disciples, Mary, Jesus' brothers, and others like me.

It was a warm Sunday morning in June. Summer was coming upon us and it promised to be a hot one. We had gathered together to pray and sing, remembering that joyous Sunday when Jesus had risen from the dead. Peter, as was now his role, was leading us in the singing. The room was warm with so many people gathered together. All of a sudden, a cool breeze began to blow. Then the room was filled with a sound like a mighty wind. Mystified, we all looked toward Peter who was standing at the front of the room, his eyes lifted toward heaven, a glorious smile on his face. Tongues of fire began shooting around the room landing on Peter, then on others. I watched in amazement as each person began praising

God in an ecstatic language, unknown to the speaker. People were laughing and shouting, some praising God on their knees, others standing with their arms outstretched toward heaven. Then the fire touched me. It cooled me on the outside and warmed my heart on the inside. I felt joy bubble up from within my spirit, a joy that was so intense I wanted to let it out. I, too, began to praise God. A language began to pour out of my mouth; a beautiful, heavenly language.

I don't know how long this continued. The intensity grew as we felt God's Holy Spirit baptize us with the most amazing love that we had ever felt. Our joy could not be contained in the house, so we ran outside praising God in all of our different languages. Surprisingly, a crowd of men had gathered outside the house. They had heard the sound of the mighty wind and had come seeking the source.

We were quite a sight, drunk with the joy of the Holy Spirit. We were laughing, singing, and praising God —all in these beautiful, diverse languages. Some of the men were laughing at us, thinking that we were drunk on wine. Others were perplexed, wondering how these poor Galileans and others had learned to speak their languages. Since it had been a holiday, there were God-fearing Jews from every country under heaven.

As the crowd grew, we moved to an open area near the temple. Peter stood on a portico and addressed the crowd. *"Fellow Jews and all of you who live in Jerusalem, let me explain this to you; listen carefully to what I say. These men are not drunk, as you suppose. It's only nine in the morning! No, this is what was spoken by the prophet Joel:*

'In the last days, God says,
I will pour out my Spirit on all people,

Your sons and daughters will prophesy,
your young men will see visions,
your old men will dream dreams'" (Acts 2:14-17 NIV).

The crowd quieted down as Peter began to share how the prophecy of Joel had now come to pass. He then preached Jesus, crucified and raised from the dead. The Spirit of God was so powerful that three thousand men were added to our number on that one day.

How the direction of my life changed on that fateful day that I was honored to help Jesus carry His cross. Now, I am compelled to share the gospel with my family and friends. I must return to my home in Cyrene, to my wife and sons, Rufus and Alexander. I have very good news to bring back to them from God's Holy Land, the Land of Israel, and God's Holy Son, Jesus the Christ.

He's Alive!

Questions

These questions are written to help you take your own journey to meet Jesus in a personal way. Only a sample of the stories have questions to go with them, but this will get you started on a very exciting adventure. Read the passages and answer the questions before you read the story. God's Word always comes first. Put yourself in each story based on the scriptures. There are no right answers. Jesus meets all of us in a unique and completely personal way.

James, the Brother of Jesus
1) Matthew 1:25. Why does scripture lead you to believe there may have been other children?
2) Luke 2:33-35. How does this scripture indicate that Joseph would not be around during Jesus' ministry?
3) After Joseph died, what role do you think Jesus played in the family?
4) How do you think the family felt when Jesus left to fulfill his ministry?
5) What were some possible events that James experienced or heard about as a part of the family? John 2:1-12; John 2:14-16; Luke 4:16-32.
6) Mark 3:20, 21. How did the family feel about all of this?
7) Matthew 12:46-50; Mark 3:31-33; Luke 8:19-21. What did the family decide to do? What happened? Do you

think Mary heard what Jesus said? Did they protect her?
8) Where did Jesus go from there? Matthew 13:1, 2.
9) Matthew 13:53-58; Mark 6:1-6. What did the people of
Nazareth think about Jesus?
10) John 7:1-10. Why were Jesus brothers taunting him?
Did they go to the festival? Why?
11) John 7:11-13; John14-52. Do you think the brothers
heard about Jesus or even saw him when they got to the
festival? Why?
12) Why do you think Mary was at the Passover by herself? Where was her family?
13) How long do you think it was before the family
heard that Jesus had been crucified? What did they think
when they heard? Do you think they were worried about
Mary?
14) 1 Corinthians 15:7. What do you think happened
when Jesus appeared to James? How would you feel if
you were James?

Read *James, the Brother of Jesus*

The Baptist
1) Luke 1. How did the story of John and Jesus intersect?
How were they related? Do you think they knew each
other? Why?
2) Luke 2:41-52. Picture John and Jesus possibly being
together in Jerusalem for this journey. Why do you think
they were together? As young boys, how would they
entertain themselves? What happened to Jesus? How did
the family deal with this?
3) Luke 1:15-17. What did the angel tell Zacharias about
John? What did the Old Testament say? Malachi 3:1
4) Matthew 3:2-12; Luke 3:7-17; John 1:19-28. Describe

John. How was he different that Jesus? What did he preach? What did the people think about him?
5) Matthew 3:13-17. As a witness, describe John's meeting with Jesus by the river. What do you think went through John's mind during this encounter? Why did he agree to baptize Jesus?

Read *The Baptist*

The Calling of Simon and Andrew
1) John 1:29-42. Who were two of John's disciples who followed Jesus? Why do you think they left John to follow him?
2) Luke 5:1-11. Picture yourself on the boat with Simon and Andrew. What was the weather like? The smell of the sea? Describe it. Who do you see standing on the shore? Why do you think Simon responded the way he did?

Read *The Calling of Simon and Andrew*

The Paralytic
1) Matthew 9:1-8; Mark 2:1-12; Luke 5:17-26. Think of a group of guys or gals in your life who might have the "chutzpah" (The Yiddish word that means courage or daring) to do something like this.
2) Why do you think the man is paralyzed? Is it physical or mental? Why were the Pharisees so angry with Jesus?

Read *The Paralytic*

The Calling of Levi
1) Matthew 9:9-13. What do you know about tax collectors? Why were the Pharisees so upset with Jesus? (Again!)

Did they have a right to be? (In their mind?) What did Jesus say in Matthew 9:13? Does that still apply to us today?

2) Mark 2:13-17. Where did Levi live? Picture him behind his little kiosk. What do you see? How long did it take Levi to get up and follow Jesus? What could he have thought to himself? What did Jesus say to the Pharisees in the Mark account?

3) Luke 5:27-32. How was this account similar to the one in Mark?

4) Why do you think Jesus called Levi (Matthew). For what purpose?

Read *The Calling of Levi*

The Wedding at Cana

1) John 1. Who did Jesus call as his disciples according to this chapter?

2) John 2:1-12. Who came to the wedding with Jesus? Why do you think this was Jesus first miracle? Why do you think John was the only one to record this miracle?

3) Picture Jesus joining at the celebration. Is he laughing? dancing? mingling?

Read *The Wedding at Cana*

Andrew and the Boy with the Loaves and Fishes.
1) Matthew 14:13-21; Mark 6:30-44; Luke 9:10-17; John 6:1-15.

2) Which books talk about Jesus getting away by himself? With his disciples? Why did the disciples need to get away? What happened with the disciples in the beginning of Luke 9? What had Jesus heard in Matthew

14:13?

3) If there were 5,000 men, how many women and children, also?

4) Imagine yourself sitting among the crowd. How were you feeling? What did you see?

5) In John 6, where did Jesus go when it was over? Why? In the Matthew account? What happened then?

Read *Andrew and the Boy with the Loaves and Fishes.*

Leah

1) Mark 5:21-43; Luke 8:40-56; Matthew 9:18-26.

2) This is a tale of a woman and a young girl. How do their stories interact? As a Jewish woman, why do you think her ailment was so detrimetal to her life?

3) In the Mark and Matthew account, we read what the woman was thinking. What was that? How do you think Mark and Matthew knew her thoughts? How difficult was it for her to tell her story to Jesus?

4) Picture yourself as this woman. What do you see, feel, and hear as you try to get to Jesus?

5) Imagine Jesus turning and looking directly at you. What does he say to you? What do you think happens next?

Read *Leah*

The Parable of the Workers in the Vineyard.

1) Matthew 20:1-16. Who represents the landowner? What does the Vineyard represent?

2) What was the scripture right before this? Matthew 19:30. How does this parable describe God's grace? How different do you think this is compared to the trad-

itional Jewish thought about rewards?

Read *The Parable of the Workers in the Vineyard*

The Prostitute

1) John 8:1-11. Picture this story in your mind. This can get personal. We have all been "caught" in our sins at one time or the other.
2) How can hypocrisy destroy the church?
3) Jesus shows grace, *but* what does he tell the woman?

Read *The Prostitute*

The Banquet

1) Luke 14:7-24
2) This story would be received by the Pharisees as laughable, ludicrous, and impossible. What do you think?
3) What is Jesus teaching us in this parable?

Read *The Banquet*

The Ten Lepers

1) Luke 17:11-19
2) There were other accounts that describe Jesus healing a leper. Luke 5:12-16; Mark 1:40-45; Matthew 8:1-4
3) What did the man say to Jesus in all of these accounts? What did Jesus say?
4) What was different about the Luke 17 account? Who were these men?
5) When were they healed?
6) Who came back to thank Jesus? What happened to him? How did the other nine miss out?

Read *The Ten Lepers*

The Woman at the Well

1) John 4:1-42
2) Where was Jesus in the story? What time of day?
3) What was special about this well?
4) Why was the woman surprised that Jesus asked her for water?
5) What was different between Jacob's water and the water that Jesus offered?
6) The woman got into a theological discussion with Jesus. What were some of her questions? What were his answers?
7) Jesus told the woman that he was the Messiah. She was the first person that he told. Why a woman? Why a Samaritan? Why someone like her?
8) What went through the disciple's minds when they saw Jesus speaking to this woman?

Read *The Woman at the Well*

The Blind Man

1) Luke 18:35-43; Matthew 20:29-34; Mark 10:46-52
2) What are some differences in these three accounts?
3) In all three accounts Jesus says, "What do you want me to do for you? How does that speak directly to you?
4) Reread the Mark account.
5) What are some things that you learned about this man?
6) How did the crowd react to him at first? At the end?
7) What do you think happened to the man?

Read *The Blind Man*

Mary and Martha

1) Luke 10:38-42
2) How important was this family to Jesus?
3) How do you think they might have met Jesus?
4) Where did they live? How close was it to Jerusalem?
5) John 11:1-46
6) What was in Martha's mind when she sent for Jesus?
7) Why didn't he come? Why were his disciples concerned?
8) Lazarus died. What was Mary thinking? Be honest. Martha?
9) When Jesus arrived, who came out to meet him? Why not Mary?
10) Jesus and Martha had an amazing conversation. What did Jesus reveal to Martha? What did Martha believe?
11) Finally, Mary came out of the house. What did Mary do when she saw Jesus?
12) Picture yourself at the tomb. What do you see? Hear?
13) Look at Jesus. What do you see? Why do you think he cried.
14) Martha was appalled that Jesus asked for the stone to be rolled away. How do you think the crowd reacted?
15) Describe Lazarus.
16) Do you think this miracle helped or hurt Jesus' ministry?
17) John 12:1-11
18) Why do you think Mary anointed Jesus' feet with this oil? (It cost over $3,000 an ounce in our day and time).
19) Is Jesus on the receiving end of grace? Or is Mary worshipping him? What do you think?
20) What did the disciples/onlookers/Pharisees think?

What do you think? What did Jesus think?

Read *Mary and Martha*

The Transfiguration

1) Mark 9
2) What did Jesus mean my Mark 9:1?
3) Who did Jesus take to the top of the mountain with him? Why these men?
4) What do you think was the purpose of the transfiguration?
5) When you see these three men standing together (Jesus, Moses, Elijah), what do you think is the topic of their conversation?

Read *The Transfiguration*

Mary Magdalene

1) Matthew 15: 35-39
2) When did Jesus visit Magdala? (vs 39) Where was it located? What happened right before he went there? Why do you think he went?
3) Luke 8:1-3
4) From this scripture, what do you learn about Mary? Susanna? Joanna?
5) Do you think following Jesus was a problem for them? Why or why not?
6) Why did women trust Jesus?
7) These women also "provided for them out of their resources" (Luke 8:3). How did these women minister to Jesus?
8) Mary Magdalene "was a prominent disciple of Jesus

who followed him in Galilee and to Jerusalem. Except for one time, she is always listed first in groups of named female disciples" (*The Dictionary of Jesus and the Gospels, 884*)

9) Why do you think Mary Magdalene got a bad rap as an "immoral" woman?

10) Who was mentioned in every crucifixion account? Matthew 27:55-56; Mark 15:40, 41; Luke 24:10, 11; John 19:25-27.

11) Luke 23:54-56.

12) How were the women identified in this account? Who did they follow?

13) Imagine listening in on their conversation. What do you think they were saying to each other?

14) Matthew 27:61

15) Picture the two Marys sitting in front of the tomb after the stone was rolled in place. What do you see?

16) Mark 16:1-8

17) The next morning, the women got up early. What was their first concern?

18) What did they see when they arrived at the tomb?

19) Put yourself in their place. What are they thinking?

20) John 20:1-18

21) How is it different from the Mark account?

22) Why do you think Jesus appeared to Mary Magdalene first?

Read *Mary Magdalene*

Write Your Own Story

Pick One Of These Or One Of Your Own.

The Stories

Jesus Walks on Water (Matthew 14:22-33)
Jesus in the Boat and the Storm (Matthew 8:23-27)
The Boy with the Evil Spirit (Luke 9:37-43)
The Widow's Mite (Luke 21:1-4)
Jesus Blesses the Children (Mark 10:13-16
The Centurion's Servant (Matthew 8:5-13)
Jesus Restores Two Demon-possessed Men (Matthew 8:28-32)
The Healing of an Epileptic Boy (Matthew 17:14-21)
Jesus Heals a Deaf and Mute Man (Mark 7:31-36)

Before You Write Your Story

1) Pray that God will take you into the story to make it yours.
2) Open your heart and mind to his voice.
3) Choose your story.
4) See if there are other versions in the gospels. Read those. Copy the story(s) from the scripture into your notebook.

5) If there is dialogue in the scripture story, use that. If there are other translations, you can use those words, also.

6) Choose which character you are.

7) If the character does not have a name, choose one.

8) Write in the first person. (i.e. My name is_____)

Overall picture:

1) What does the passage tell you about the story?

2) Where does the passage take place? Check your map to see if you can find the place.

3) What is happening in the story?

4) When does it take place? Day? Night? Season? The story may or may not let you know. Look at the story in context. Read the chapters before and after. Where was Jesus? What was happening?

5) How does God work in this story?

Focus in on the characters (You and others)

1) How are you feeling in the story? The other people in the story?

2) What are you seeing? Hearing? Touching? Smelling?

3) What is your experience with the Master?

4) What does he look like?

5) What is he doing?

6) How are people reacting to him?

7) At a crucial part of the story, Jesus will look directly at you. (This is the BEST part!) What does he say to you? What is the expression on his face? Describe his eyes. What happens to you? How do you feel? Can you put that feeling into words? Ask God to give you the words.

Make It Yours

The following stories were written by two precious

friends of mine. These two friends have taught me so much about Jesus and how he can truly change a person's life. I wanted to include their stories in this book. Each woman wrote their story from a different place. As you read, they will take you to Jesus.

Jesus and the Children

By Amber Crawford

When Jesus saw what was happening, he was angry with his disciples. He said to them, "Let the children come to me. Don't stop them! For the Kingdom of God belongs to those who are like these children. I tell you the truth, anyone who doesn't receive the Kingdom of God like a child will never enter it." Then he took the children in his arms and placed his hands on their heads and blessed them. Mark 10: 13-16

Today is the day. I arose early, earlier than usual. I'm not even sure I slept last night. I'm excited, nervous, hopeful, and anxious all at once. My husband came home from work yesterday afternoon smiling the biggest smile. At supper, he told the children and me about a man that he saw in town today, the man known as Jesus. He told us that he watched as Jesus touched an old, crippled beggar, known to all in town, and instantly the old man stood without help. He said he even leaped, danced, and cried tears of joy.

After witnessing this miracle, my husband and friends were amazed. They decided that the following morning, each of them would bring their wife and children and go into town together to find the Healer. All of our families were fairly healthy, save for some smaller issues. Brandon and Stephanie's son, Braydon, had a stutter, Crystal and Jason's son, Waylon, had frequent night terrors, and our Norah had a lazy eye. Although she was otherwise healthy, we knew eventually she could lose her vision. Sometimes other children made fun of her. The men had decided we would take the children to Jesus and ask Him to bless them.

It was time. I woke my husband and went to prepare breakfast while he woke the children. After breakfast, we hurried to meet the others. Everyone was nervous and excited as we walked into town looking for Jesus. Would He welcome us? Would He scoff and turn us away? Was He even the One or had the men been mistaken? As the morning passed, we became discouraged. He was nowhere to be found. Had He already left town? Was He ever really there?

As lunchtime grew closer, the children began to grumble and complain. We considered giving up for the day. Then suddenly, we spotted a crowd of men resting under a tree. In the center of the group was Jesus. When our husbands saw Him, they grabbed the children. The other wives and I hurried behind them.

As we got closer, I could feel peace and kindness in the air around this man called Jesus. The men, holding the children in their arms, knelt on one knee and bowed their heads.

My husband was the one to speak. "Rabbi," he said. "We saw what you did yesterday for the old beggar. Please, if you are willing...."

Before he could finish speaking one of the men around Jesus stood up. "Have you no respect? The Lord is resting. Go, leave Him alone."

"The day has been long," said another as he stood also.

Soon all were standing, scolding us for disturbing Jesus and forcing us back. We were crushed with disappointment. The children clutched tightly to their fathers in fear of the men's aggression.

As we turned in defeat heading home, we heard a voice above all the others. *"Let the children come to me. Do not stop them! For the Kingdom of God belongs to those who are like these children. I tell you the truth, anyone who doesn't receive the kingdom of God like a child will never enter it."*

As the men parted for us, I looked up and my eyes met His. I felt an overwhelming sense of joy, peace, love, and hope. His eyes were full of compassion, understanding, and acceptance. Love seemed to radiate from Him, drawing us in closer.

When we reached Him, He lovingly took Norah into His arms, placing a gentle kiss on the top of her head. Instantly she stopped crying and all fear left her innocent face. He sat down under a tree, Norah still in His arms. The way they looked at each other was as if He was her best friend. There was nothing but contentment and peace.

He motioned for the boys to come, and they were placed on either side of Him. He wrapped His arms around all three of the children. He spoke to each child, asking them questions and then telling them stories that made them laugh.

I stood in awe as the Lamb of God held my precious child, loving on her as if she were His own child. Then it hit me—she is! A tear rolled down my cheek as I watched Jesus touch their heads one by one and pray blessings over them.

Afterwards, Norah came running to me, a huge smile on her face. I noticed her eye was perfect. I hit my knees, wrapped my arms around her, and thanked God for His blessing. We then realized that Brayden's stutter was gone. A few days later, Waylon's night-terrors were gone, also.

The Son of God came, and I was blessed to see Him face to face.

The Sower

By Lindsey Gammill

One day Jesus told a story in the form of a parable to a large crowd that had gathered from many towns to hear him: 5"A farmer went out to plant his seed. As he scattered it across his field, some seed fell on a footpath, where it was stepped on, and the birds ate it. 6Other seed fell among rocks. It began to grow, but the plant soon wilted and died for lack of moisture. 7Other seed fell among thorns that grew up with it and choked out the tender plants. 8Still other seed fell on fertile soil. This seed grew and produced a crop that was a hundred times as much as had been planted!" When he had said this, he called out, "Anyone with ears to hear should listen and understand."

9His disciples asked him what this parable meant. 10He replied, "You are permitted to understand the secrets8:10a Greek mysteries. of the Kingdom of God. But I use parables to teach the others so that the Scriptures might be fulfilled:

'When they look, they won't really see.

When they hear, they won't understand.'8:10b Isa 6:9 (Greek version).

11"This is the meaning of the parable: The seed is God's word.12The seeds that fell on the footpath represent those who hear the message, only to have the devil come and take it away from their hearts and prevent them from believing and being saved. 13The seeds on the rocky soil represent those who hear the message and receive it with joy. But since they don't have deep roots, they believe for a while, then they fall away when they face temptation. 14The seeds that fell among the thorns represent those who hear the message, but all too quickly the message is crowded out by the cares and riches and pleasures of this life. And so they never grow into maturity. 15And the seeds that fell on the good soil represent honest, good-hearted people who hear God's word, cling to it, and patiently produce a huge harvest (Luke 8:4-15; Matthew 13:1-23).

I n this story, I am James. I am intrigued by my brother, Jesus, who always seems to know the answer or has the right thing to say. This is a day unlike any other. Jesus walks out of the house and goes to sit by the sea. I follow him. A multitude of people gather around as Jesus starts telling parables.

He tells a parable about a farmer who sows many seeds. There are four different types of seeds. The disciples came up to him later and asked, *"Why are you speaking to us in parables?"* His answer was directed at me.

"You are permitted to understand the secrets of the kingdom of God. I use parables to teach the others so that the scripture might be fulfilled; seeing they may not see, and hearing they may not understand" (Luke 8:10).

The parable of the farmer scattering seed (the sower) takes place in Galilee. In the parable, it's a hot day—so it's summertime more than likely. We listen in awe. He speaks softly, and I can feel God's presence. Jesus is wearing a tan robe with a white tunic underneath.

As he addresses the multitude, I feel in tune with God and content to listen to my brother speak and preach. I smell the sea in the breeze and feel the warm air on my skin.

I think about the seeds that were scattered and the meaning of the parable. The seed is God's word. He taught this parable to explain how important the state of our heart is to receive the gospel. Our salvation is proved by our choices and actions after hearing the gospel.

Bibles

Unless otherwise indicated, Scripture quotations are taken from The Holy Bible, New King James Version. Copyright © 1979, 1980, 1982 by Thomas Nelson, Inc.

Scripture quotations marked "NLT" are taken from the Holy Bible, New Living Translation. Copyright © 1996 by Tyndale Charitable Trust.

Also quoted, Scriptures taken from the Holy Bible, New International Version (NIV). Copyright © 1973, 1978, 1984 International Bible Society. Used by permission of Zondervan Bible Publishers.

Scriptures quoted in To See Him Face to Face are printed in italics.

Acknowledgement

Lord, it's been almost twenty years now. Thank you for sending me on this amazing journey into the lives of real people in the Bible. I am grateful to Tricia McCary Rhodes who taught me in her book, *The Soul at Rest,* a different way to look at the scriptures. It was my friends, Emma, Ruby, and Jean who read the stories and encouraged me. I was able to publish the stories before my mother died, and she was so proud to have them in a real book. Many of my friends have now gone on to be with the Lord. They have been such an important part of my Christian walk. I can't wait to reconnect someday.

God has blessed me with an incredible and loving family. Thank you, Preston, for fifty years of precious and unconditional love and support. To Stacey, Robert, Shane, Stephanie, and Starr—you are my inspiration. To Kate, Saylor, Preston, Asher, Silas, and Slaton—you are the main reason that I wanted to publish this book—to bequeath to you my love for Jesus. To Mother—thank you for believing in me and being my proofreader. To Daddy—your love for me made it so easy to undersatnd God the Father's love. You were my Abba. To Marian and Ray—thank you for embracing me as part of your family.

Soli Deo Gloria

About The Author

Cindy Hamilton

Cindy Hamilton is a retired school counselor who has turned her love for Jesus, her family, and writing into captivating first person stories from the New Testament. As a Bible teacher for many years, her imagination and the reality of what it means to be a Christ-follower have led to a unique relationship with Jesus. She lives with her husband and two dogs, Max and Wynna, in the small town of Lonoke, Arkansas.

Books By This Author

Anna's Chair

Flesh-and-blood enemies. Evil rulers? Unseen world. Mighty powers in this dark world?

Sixteen-year-old Anna James and her best friends, Grace and Shelby, are just livin' life—texting, Instagram, Snapchat—tenth grade ordinary. That is until three missionary kids move into their town and flip their safe world upside down.

What is it about these three? Miracles happen when they come around . . . strange occurrences . . . God's supernatural. They remind Anna of someone. Someone she'd met years ago. No one believed her back then. Would anyone believe her now?

Maybe, there is a world out there different from her own. Who knew?

Printed in Great Britain
by Amazon

81869740R00153